STAR WARS INSIDER

THE HIGH REPUBLIC

STARLIGHT STORIES

STAR WARS INSIDER
THE HIGH REPUBLIC

STARLIGHT STORIES

Tales from a more civilized age...

This volume features original fiction chronicling the days of the High Republic centuries prior to the fall and purge of the Jedi Order.

The stories feature heroic new Jedi and a new central setting, the Starlight Beacon, a space station located on the galactic frontier, as we meet the personnel and staff in tales that are both epic and personal.

Additionally, story architects Claudia Gray, Justina Ireland, Daniel José Older, Cavan Scott, and Charles Soule discuss their work on building the bold new vision for the *Star Wars* galaxy.

TITAN EDITORIAL

Editor Jonathan Wilkins
Art Director Oz Browne
Group Editor Jake Devine
Senior Creative Editor David Leach
Sub-editor Phoebe Hedges
Assistant Editor Louis Yamani
Editorial Assistant Ibraheem Kazi
Designers Donna Askem, Dan Bura & David Colderley
Head Of Production Kevin Wooff
Production Manager Jackie Flook
Production Controllers Caterina Falqui & Kelly Fenlon
Publicity Manager Will O'Mullane
Publicist Caitlin Storer
Publicity & Sales Coordinator Alexandra Iciek
Digital & Marketing Manager Jo Teather
Marketing Coordinator Lauren Noding
Sales & Circulation Manager Steve Tothill
Head Of Rights Rosanna Anness
Rights Executive Pauline Savourè
Head Of Creative & Business Development Duncan Baizley
Publishing Directors Ricky Claydon & John Dziewiatkowski
Chief Operating Officer Andrew Sumner
Publishers Vivian Cheung & Nick Landau

DISTRIBUTION
U.S. Distribution: Penguin Random House
U.K. Distribution: MacMillan Distribution
Direct Sales Market: Diamond Comic Distributor
General Inquires: customerservice@titanpublishingusa.com

First edition: November 2024

Star Wars Insider: The High Republic: Starlight Stories is published by Titan Magazines, a division of Titan Publishing Group Limited, 144 Southwark Street, London, SE1 0UP
Printed in China.
For sale in the U.S., Canada, U.K., and Eire
ISBN: 9781787745209
Titan Authorized User. TMN 4767

A CIP catalogue record for this title is available from the British Library.

10 9 8 7 6 5 4 3 2 1

LUCASFILM EDITORIAL
Senior Editor Brett Rector
Art Director Troy Alders
Creative Director Michael Siglain
Story Group Leland Chee, Pablo Hidalgo, Emily Shkoukani, Matt Martin, Kate Izquierdo
Creative Art Manager Phil Szostak
Asset Management Chris Argyropoulos, Gabrielle Levenson, Sarah Williams, Bryce Pinkos, Erik Sanchez, Elinor De La Torre, Jackey Cabrera, Shahana Alam
Special Thanks: Samantha Keane, Kevin Pearl and Eugene Paraszczuk

TITAN MAGAZINES

Disney · LUCASFILM

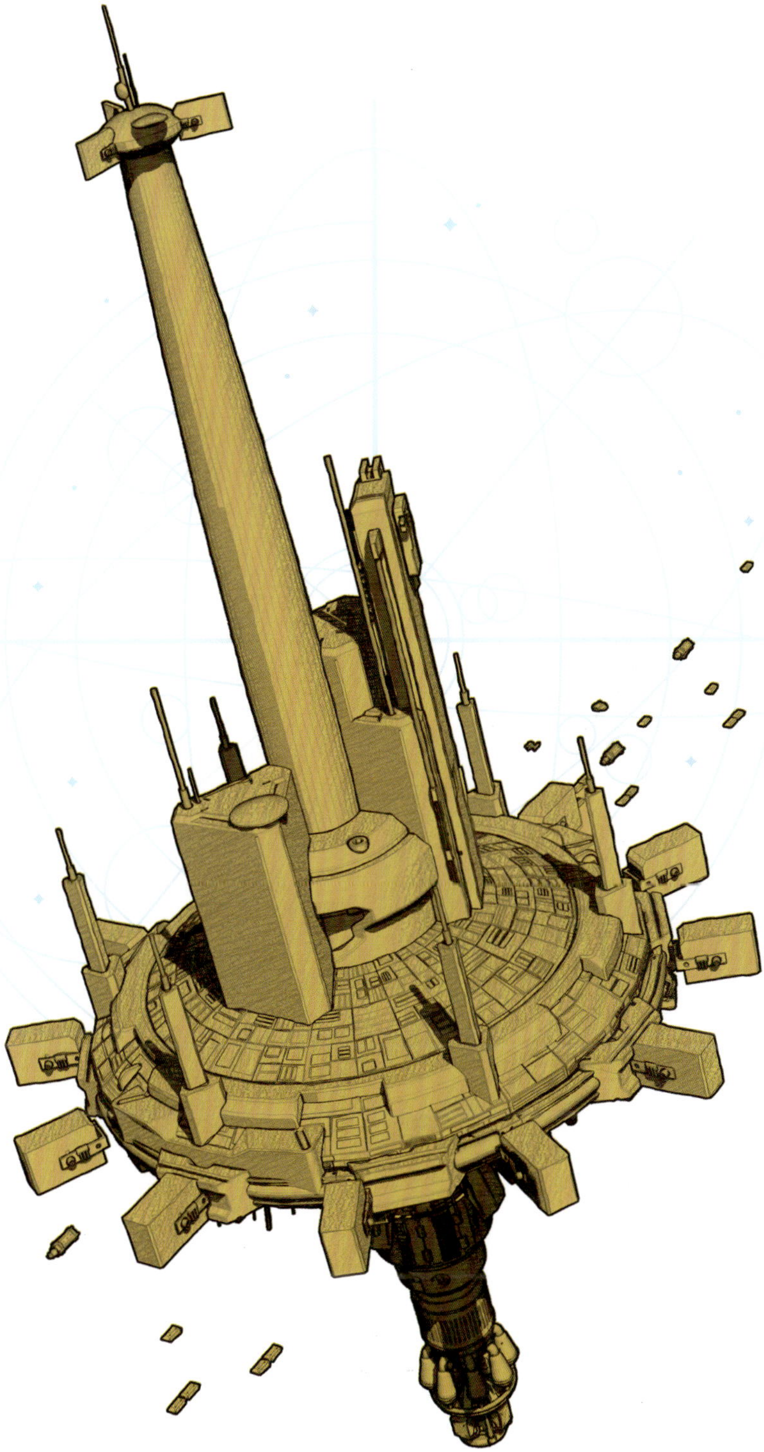

STAR WARS
THE HIGH REPUBLIC

CONTENTS

Go Together

PART ONE

By Charles Soule

The Outer Rim.
The Starlight Beacon.

Joss Adren lifted a pile of dirty, grease-stained clothes from the floor. He considered, then balled them up and shoved them in the sack he was using as luggage, atop the clean clothes he'd already thrown in.

He glanced around the bedroom. Nothing else he needed. He always traveled light when working.

"All packed," he said, throwing the sack on the bed, next to several small cases holding his wife's clothes and assorted sundries, packed hours earlier—and he'd bet a hundred credits there wasn't a dirty sock anywhere in them.

"You ready?" Joss asked her, calling into the tiny living room that formed the rest of their personal space aboard the Starlight Beacon.

It was gorgeously designed—everything on the station was—but space in space would always be at a premium.

"Maybe we can get something to eat before we get out of here," he added.

The canteens on Starlight Beacon were excellent, serving dishes from all over the Outer Rim, to showcase the cultures that comprised this far-off edge of the Republic. The principle carried through the whole station; its structure used metallic ores from many different worlds, and housed craftspeople, contractors, and staff from planets throughout the Outer Rim Territories.

Starlight Beacon was a wonder. Joss had never seen anything like it, and his career had taken him across half the galaxy.

He and Pikka were project managers, specialists in bringing large-scale construction jobs to completion. They worked out last-minute bugs in the code, silenced rattling pipes, dealt with coolant leaks.

They'd spent the last few months getting Starlight Beacon ready for its formal dedication... but now the last bolt was bolted and the last weld was welded. Even the biological reserves were fully stocked. They felt lonely without the tourists expected to come for a glimpse of the biodiversity of worlds like Mon Cala and Felucia... but they were gorgeous and lush all the same, even the desert biomes.

Starlight Beacon was, at last, complete, and Joss and Pikka Adren had played a big part in making that happen. Reason enough to be proud. Joss didn't consider himself overly emotional, but this was a special place—emblematic of all the Galactic Republic could and should be.

But just then, Joss couldn't wait to get the hell off the thing. His wife had planned a vacation for them both, with a surprise destination. Knowing Pikka, it would be somewhere spectacular.

They had to catch the next ship heading back to Coruscant, and Pikka had made it very clear they couldn't be late. So it was extremely *unclear* why, now that Joss was finally packed and ready, she was completely absorbed in the datapad she was holding, tapping away at its keys, her face screwed up in the focused way he... well, he liked it very much. He was crazy about this woman. It was mostly her mind—she saw the galaxy in a way he didn't, which meant she constantly surprised and delighted him—but he loved her small-but-not delicate body too, and her weird curly hair. Pikka was just... home. No matter where they were, she was home.

"Didn't you tell me that under no circumstances could I make us late?" Joss said.

"Hmm?" Pikka said, not looking up from the datapad.

"What are you reading?" he asked. "A steamy Zeltron novel?"

"I wish," she said.

She lifted the datapad. It displayed energy usage across the entirety of Starlight Beacon, power ebbing and flowing along thousands of kilometers of wires and conduits. A web of light in the rough shape of the station—a gigantic central sphere with tower-like extensions at either pole.

"Okay..." Joss said, not understanding.

"Look," Pikka said, and pointed at single, tiny point of data. "That's too high."

Joss squinted at the datapad.

"Hmm," he said. "Yeah. Not by much, though."

"Not by much. But by some. And a minute ago it was half a percent less."

Joss knew what his wife was thinking: they'd been hired to optimize Starlight Beacon. While they had done that job, and this little tiny power surge was barely even noticeable, his brilliant wife had noticed it. And now he had too.

He sighed.

"Let's go figure it out."

She grinned.

Pikka headed for the door, clearly expecting Joss to follow, the idea that they might be late for their transportation Coreward and the subsequent vacation apparently gone from her mind.

Joss sighed again. His wife did love a puzzle.

***

I love puzzles, Pikka thought, moving purposefully along a corridor, her attention mostly on the datapad in her hand, though she had that sense of Joss following not too far behind. She always knew when her husband was near—either she felt good, warm and strong, or she didn't. That simple.

It could also just be that he made a lot of noise. Joss was not a small man. It wouldn't surprise her to learn that one of his parents was a reek.

She turned a corner, and almost collided with Shai Tennem, arguably the last person on the station she would want to see. Shai was a Bith, a particularly particular Bith, charged with overseeing Starlight Beacon's construction by the Chancellor of the Republic, Lina Soh herself. He was legendary (or notorious) for his incredibly exacting standards. He would find an energy transfer abnormality *quite vexing,* no matter how insignificant.

Even worse—Shai Tennem was not alone. He was leading what looked like a tour group. It snapped together in Pikka's mind—yes, Joss had mentioned this. A number of Republic dignitaries had come to see the finished station a few weeks before it came fully online. She recognized Admiral Kronara, a high-ranking officer in the Republic Defense Coalition. As for the others...

Jedi. In robes of white and gold, with filigree shapes embossed here and there, and holstered lightsabers at their hips or slung across their torsos. A tall human woman with yellow hair, walking alongside a dark-haired man with caramel skin. A curved-skulled, wide-eyed Ithorian. A female Duros. Another human, hair in long, beautiful gray braids, beside a tall, golden-furred Wookiee—Pikka didn't know there *were* any Wookiee Jedi.

Behind closed doors, Joss called them 'space wizards.' Jedi had strange powers and abilities, and Pikka imagined they could probably use that magic to do a lot of harm, if they wanted to. In her experience, powerful people used that power to advance their own interests. But not the Jedi Order. They were good people. Incredibly, unassailably good, dedicated to helping people.

"Ah, Mrs. Adren," Shai said, in his clipped, reedy voice. "Lovely to see you. I'm just showing the Republic emissaries around the station."

Tennem turned to face the Jedi.

"My friends, meet Pikka and Joss Adren. They were instrumental in ensuring Starlight Beacon's on-time, error-free construction."

"Pleased to meet you," Joss said. He even gave a little wave.

What is he thinking? Pikka thought, the datapad in her hand feeling hot.

"Likewise," said the blonde Jedi, smiling. "Thank you for your work. This place is incredible."

"Why don't you join us?" Shai said to Joss. "I'm sure you can offer insights about Starlight Beacon's systems our guests would find interesting."

Pikka chanced a glance at her datapad—that small bump in power usage she'd noticed was on its way to becoming a surge. She gritted her teeth.

The Wookiee Jedi was looking at her. He cocked his head.

Is he reading my mind? She thought.

"Joss, we should probably go," Pikka said, hoping Joss could read her mind too. "We don't want to be late."

He threw her a quick glance.

"That's right," Joss said, turning to the admiral. "Actually, we're hitching a ride with you all when you go."

Kronara acknowledged this with a tight nod.

"We're on our way to the hangar now. Joss, was it? I'd get down there soon, or we'll leave without you."

Shai Tennem spoke up.

"That's perfect. Come along with us, you two. Porter droids can bring your things from your quarters."

Pikka's heart rate spiked. She would have to explain the situation right in front of Shai, wouldn't she? In front of these important people, she would have to embarrass herself, and the station administrator. Even worse, *this could actually be a real problem*. They needed to leave, to learn whether this power issue was more than a glitch.

Out of the corner of her eye, she saw the Wookiee turn to the gray-haired Jedi and murmur quietly in its language. The woman raised a hand.

"Actually, Administrator Tennem," the Jedi said, "Shouldn't the Adrens enjoy their last moments on the station before they depart? It sounds like they've already done their part for Starlight Beacon."

Shai nodded deferentially.

"As you say, Master Assek," he said.

"Right," Pikka said, pulling at Joss' arm. "Nice to meet all of you."

The Jedi parted as they passed. Pikka thought she felt her skin tingle. Probably just her imagination.

They turned a corner, and she showed Joss the datapad.

"It's getting worse," she said, her voice quiet.

Joss looked. He frowned.

"This way," he said, and set off down the corridor.

***

Joss kept maps in his head; one reason he was so good at his job. He studied worksites until he had the systems and sub-systems memorized, the way surgeons knew the bodies of their patients. Starlight Beacon was no exception.

Ever since Pikka showed him the anomalous power reading, his brain had churned through that mental map. He was zeroing in, seeing the station in his head, and it brought him...

Here. Conduit 398-GX14, situated behind an access panel near the entrance to Starlight's Jedi temple.

"Just jumped another twenty percent," Pikka said.

Joss frowned. This wasn't quite at 'evacuate the station' level yet, but if it kept building...

He levered off the casing to Conduit 398-GX14, dropped to one knee and peered inside, catching a whiff of hot, overstressed metal. He pushed aside a few bundles of wiring, and immediately saw the problem.

A meter along the conduit, a resistor hub had burned out. It was acting like a dam within the power distributors, not letting energy past, just collecting it and boosting it. Joss had seen this before—probably a poorly seated wire. Whether originally a mistake by an assembly droid or a technician, one tiny error had created a feedback loop, cycling and building, accelerating.

And this particular conduit was an offshoot that led directly to the main reactor system, which meant...

"We have to fix this *now*," Joss said, matter-of-fact. "It'll short out the whole damn station."

"Can we cut power to this section?" Pikka asked. "Buy some time?"

"We don't have authorization now that our contract's up, and we've only got about thirty seconds before the surge overwhelms the resistor hub. But I can fix this. I know a trick—I can create a temporary circuit to dissipate the energy. We'll be okay."

Joss pulled out one of the spanners he kept in his worksuit pretty much all the time. You never knew when you'd need a spanner. He reached into the conduit... and stopped. He flexed his fingers, tried elongating his hand, tried... Joss' arms were as big as the rest of him—good for construction work. Good for all kinds of work. Scars on his knuckles could speak to that. But they were bad at fitting inside small electrical conduits.

"It's no good. My arm's too big."

He looked at Pikka. Fifteen seconds now, maybe.

"Give it to me," she said. "Tell me what to do."

He didn't argue. Just handed her the spanner.

"You'll need to do this by feel," Joss said, as his wife knelt and reached her arm into the opening. "But don't touch the conduit walls. You could absorb the charge, electrocute yourself."

Pikka gave him a frustrated look.

"Joss... I don't know what I'm doing. I'm systems. You're the mechanic."

Her voice was steady—anyone but her husband would think Pikka Adren didn't have an ounce of fear in her body.

He put his hand on her arm.

"I'll guide you. I'll feel it when you get to the right spot."

Pikka reached slowly forward into the conduit. Then, suddenly, the slightest impact, transmitted along her arm to his fingertips—she'd found the hub.

"Okay," he said. "There's a little nub at the end of the spanner. Lock onto it, then a twist to the right. Quick, short. Turn it for this long, no more, no less."

He increased the pressure with his index finger for a second and a half, then pulled it away.

"You get it?"

"Yeah," she said.

Joss hoped so. And if it didn't work... well, he was touching her. If the built-up energy discharged into her body, they'd go together.

But they didn't. The corridor felt suddenly still, serene. A sense of a vanished vibration, too subtle to hear until it was no longer there.

"I think I got it," Pikka said.

"We're alive," Joss answered. "The lights are still on. Both good signs."

Pikka carefully pulled her arm from the conduit. Joss bent to look, and yes, the problem was solved.

He looked at his wife.

"If we'd headed to the hangar like we planned... if you hadn't run that last scan of the station's systems..."

"I know," Pikka said.

She leaned forward and kissed him, a nice hit on his lips, not too long, not too short.

"You're a very lucky man."

She snapped her fingers.

"Come on," she said. "We have a ship to catch."

***

The *Third Horizon* was an elegant vessel. An *Emissary*-class cruiser, shining and bright—the epitome of Republic ship design, speeding through hyperspace on its way back to Coruscant. Definitely not the worst ride the Adrens had ever taken.

Pikka was sitting in the hangar bay, finishing an incident report for Shai Tennem about the wiring issue on Starlight Beacon.

She sent it off, then looked up at Joss across the hangar, admiring one of the new Longbeams that were part of the *Third Horizon*'s complement of support vessels. Long, sleek and thin, the Longbeams could serve as passenger or cargo ships, rescue vessels, even mid-size combat craft. Joss was deep in conversation with a member of the deck crew, a blue-skinned Twi'lek. Joss laughed heartily and slapped the man on the shoulder. Pikka smiled. Joss could make friends anywhere.

A siren sounded, and a voice came across the ship's intercom system—focused and steady. She looked up, listening.

"This is Admiral Kronara. We have received a distress signal from the Hetzal system, regarding a system-wide mass casualty event. We are close enough to divert to offer assistance. Any passengers with piloting, rescue or emergency medical experience willing to aid in the relief effort, please make yourselves known to a crewmember."

The intercom fell silent, and Pikka felt the *Third Horizon* drop from hyperspace. She had no idea what a 'system-wide mass casualty event' could even be. The Republic was at peace. A supernova, maybe? What could possibly…?

The important thing was that 'system-wide' meant billions of lives. No other way to interpret it.

She sensed the telltale presence, turned her head, and there was Joss.

"We have to see if we can help," he said.

Pikka didn't even try to dissuade him. They could both fly a ship, and they had all sorts of training that could be useful in a crisis. She just nodded.

"I love you," she said. "Let's go…"

TO BE CONTINUED…

Go Together
PART TWO

By Charles Soule

A long time ago, in a galaxy far, far away....

Pikka Adren surveyed the room, sensing the comforting bulk of her husband just behind her. Joss, for once, was being quiet—a good thing, considering the people seated around the table waiting for them. They did not seem like types for idle chit-chat.

She and Joss had been on this station before. Starlight Beacon, the massive installation constructed in the Outer Rim as one of Chancellor Lina Soh's Great Works, emblematic of the Galactic Republic. But since her last time here, the path she and her husband had taken had led them to unbelievable places, and they had done things she still couldn't believe they'd achieved, or even survived. As a result they now stood in an elegantly-appointed conference chamber, summoned to some sort of debriefing with a good portion of the Republic's most senior leadership. Chancellor Soh herself sat at the head of the table, with a blonde human woman in white and gold robes to her right—Jedi Master Avar Kriss, the highest-ranking member of her Order stationed at Starlight.

Pikka knew Master Kriss from a space battle in which they had recently both participated. A space battle! What terrible sins had she committed in a former life to find herself fighting in a space battle? She and Joss were basically just high-level construction workers.They'd helped to complete Starlight Beacon, in fact.

In truth, she had no one to blame but herself. She and Joss had actually volunteered to fight at the Battle of Kur.

Remembering the feeling of that battle—the chaos, the intensity, the fear—Pikka felt herself trembling, and forced herself back to calm. Whatever the reason she and her husband had been summoned here, she and Joss had wanted to help. That was all.

On the chancellor's left, a high-ranking officer in the Republic Defense Coalition. His name was Admiral Pevel Kronara, silver-haired in a uniform of gray and blue, and Pikka knew him a little bit too. A good, straightforward, hugely competent career soldier.

The rest of the seats were occupied by a combination of government and coalition officials—she knew Senator Izzet Noor, but the others were new to her. A bunch of those gray and blue RDC uniforms, though. Pikka frowned a little. A lot of warriors for a galaxy supposedly at peace.

"Welcome," said Chancellor Soh. "Please sit. We want to get through the debriefings as soon as possible."

Joss and Pikka stepped forward, pulling out chairs and sitting down. The message they'd received, from one of Kronara's aides, was vague, only indicating that their presence was requested to help with the creation of an after-action report on the Battle of Kur. While Pikka didn't have much interest in reliving those moments, she understood the importance of passing along their impressions of the fight.

But she and her husband had figured on a quick interview with an RDC functionary, not an audience with some of the most important people in the galaxy. This felt like some sort of interrogation—or a trial! She was exhausted, Joss was too. Neither of them had slept well since Kur, and they'd probably overindulged at Starlight Beacon's dedication ceremony the night before. She felt like a shadow, barely present, her insubstantiality underscored by the brightness of everyone else in the room.

"So... good morning," Joss said. "If I'd known this would be a formal occasion, I'd have brushed my teeth. What is this, exactly?"

Pikka grimaced.

Avar Kriss grinned.

"I get it," she said. "I was up late last night myself. Quite a party. I know this isn't what any of us want to be doing this morning, but it won't take long. You were both instrumental in helping to defeat the Nihil at Kur. We have some questions about how you did it."

Pikka exchanged a glance with her husband, and then looked back at the Jedi and shrugged.

"We just tried to stay alive," she said. "Not much more to it."

"I disagree," said Admiral Kronara. "You flew one of our Longbeams, as part of a Republic Defense Coalition fleet assembled to go up against a group of Outer Rim marauders called the Nihil."

"You helped bring justice for the billions of innocent lives ended by their savage attacks," added Chancellor Soh, somberly, yet with a note of approval, of consequences duly meted out.

"Just so," Kronara agreed.

He tapped a control on the table, and a hovering comms droid projected a two-dimensional image. It was a bit crude, more graphic than realistic, but Pikka recognized what was being displayed immediately.

At her side, Joss grunted. He had recognized it too.

The Kur Nebula. And in a zone not far from its center, a vast array of warships depicted as brightly colored symbols. The Republic's forces in green—a number of RDC cruisers including Admiral Kronara's flagship, the elegant *Emissary*-class *Third Horizon*, along with a wide complement of smaller attack ships, the mid-sized Longbeams and single-pilot Incom Z-28 Skywing fighters. The Jedi cruiser *Ataraxia*, and its own spread of the small, nimble Vectors, each with a Jedi pilot at the helm, all in blue. And the Nihil in red—their ugly, blocky, spike-covered ships, each with the three glowing lightning strikes slashed across their hull. The Nihil vessels were like jagged, broken teeth in a diseased jaw.

She and Joss were somewhere in that mix too. One of those Longbeams was theirs, the *Aurora III*, with Pikka navigating and running the weapons systems and Joss in the pilot's chair. Flying, fighting, trying desperately to stay alive.

Pikka clenched her trembling hand. She could feel the weapon controls under her fingertips, see the Nihil targets on her display. Their cockpit awash in the green light of the nebula, not knowing if they'd be alive ten seconds later. She could hear Joss, shouting out—

***

"By the light… what are they doing?" Joss cried out.

Looking out from the Longbeam's cockpit, he could see one of the Nihil ships, a big, bulky thing. He thought maybe it was a converted waste hauler, and that suspicion was underscored when the ship opened its cargo compartment and released a sea of horrible sludge in its wake.

Another Longbeam and two Skywings were on the Nihil's tail, all moving at such speed that they had no opportunity to dodge. They flew straight into the cloud of awful, gray-brown filth, which was ignited by their engines, and all three Republic ships vanished into balls of flame.

What a horrible, disgusting, dishonorable way to go. And it wasn't the worst tactic the Nihil were using out here, either.

The Nihil fought like beasts, like cornered animals, trying anything they could to destroy, to kill. They used laser cannons, missiles and torpedoes, but that was just the beginning. Some of their ships were venting radioactive gas from their reactors, poisoning pilots unlucky enough to fly through it. Others, heavily armored, were actively and deliberately trying to ram into Republic ships.

Joss caught panicked reports from other pilots across the fleet. None of them were cowards—far from it—but no one had ever fought anything like this.

A proton torpedo lanced out from the Longbeam's weapons array, and a small, ugly Nihil fighter vanished."Good shot, Pikka!" Joss called back.

His wife didn't answer. Staying focused on the task at hand. That was good. They both needed to do that. He flew, she chose the targets. And it was working. As Joss looked over his tactical display, he had a sense that the Nihil were losing, slowly but surely. RDC discipline and training was overcoming the Nihil's willingness to fight dirty.

Something happened.

The red icons representing the Nihil forces began blipping in and out of existence, disappearing and reappearing. Joss slammed the heel of his hand against the console, figuring maybe there was a short—nothing like a good thump to fix a poorly seated wire—but nothing changed, except that now, Republic and Jedi ships started to disappear from the display. Not so dramatic when it was little icons on a screen, but... Joss looked up. He could see what was actually happening with his own eyes, and it was horrifying. Unbelievable. The Nihil ships making what seemed to be micro-jumps through hyperspace, tiny hops that made them impossible to target, vanishing and reappearing short distances away. And all around them, explosions blossoming against the blackness of space, as good people died trying to do the right thing.

***

Pikka looked at the projection above the conference table, remembering the horror of that moment, realizing that their enemy was capable of something they weren't, and had no way to fight.

"We still don't know how the Nihil did this," said Admiral Kronara, "but we know the tactic was devastating in the battle-space. Only the Jedi seemed able to effectively fight them off, through their enhanced reflexes and speed."

"Through the Force," Avar said.

Kronara gave a tight nod in acknowledgment, then turned back to Pikka and Joss.

"I misspoke," the admiral said. "The Jedi were not the only pilots who seemed able to counteract the Nihil micro-jumps."

He pointed, all the way down the table, right at them.

"You did it too. Your Longbeam was able to react and maneuver with precision and speed beyond that of the rest of our fleet. Where others died, you two survived. We need to know how you did it."

Pikka swallowed. She glanced at her husband.

"Would you believe we're just that good?" Joss said.

"Probably not," said Kronara.

"Maybe we used the Force," he said.

"In a way, all living things use the Force," Avar said. "But no. You didn't."

Chancellor Soh spoke, the first words she'd said since welcoming them in.

"Joss, Pikka. We need to know what you did. Was it luck, or something we can replicate? Something that might save other lives, in potential fights yet to come."

"But the Nihil are gone. All of their ships were destroyed in the battle."

"Yes," the chancellor said. "I know. Still… indulge us."

Pikka looked at Joss. He shrugged.

"Tell them," she said.

***

Joss looked at the uptight, buttoned-down, frowning faces seated around the table. The only people who seemed relaxed were the chancellor and the space wizard, which made sense—they were the most powerful people in the room. He sighed. They were stuck.

"We sliced the security systems on the Longbeam's operational code," he said. "Or, actually…"

He pointed his thumb at Pikka.

"…she did."

"Thanks a lot," his wife muttered.

"Slicing Republic military hardware carries heavy penalties," one of the RDC officials said.

"Higher than dying?" Joss shot back, heated. "Pikka and I are tinkerers. It's how we make our living. We figure out systems and think of ways to improve them. Whether it's a space station or a starship, we both like to know how stuff works. We weren't going to take one of your Longbeams into a battle unless we knew what it could do."

He looked at Pikka, nodded for her to continue.

"So, yeah. I sliced the ops code. That's all. I didn't change anything."

"Well…" Joss said.

Pikka shot him a glare, then took a deep breath. She looked up at the battle display, remembering.

***

"Uncouple the thrusters!" Joss shouted at her.

"What?" Pikka frowned.

"That thing you found in the code!" he said, as the ship jerked sharply, probably narrowly avoiding some version of a hot, agonizing death.

She realized what he meant. When she had sliced into the Longbeam's code back on the *Third Horizon* before they'd taken it out, she'd seen that all its thrusters were computer controlled, linked together to ensure smooth maneuvering. But it was possible, with a few elegant shortcuts, to unlink them, so each thruster could operate independently, under manual control.

Pikka entered the commands, and suddenly the ship's handling felt… looser. More open.

"All right," she heard Joss say. "That'll work. Let's see what this thing can actually do."

The Longbeam moved again, sidestepping, skipping across space. It felt different, alive in a way that it hadn't before.

Joss grunted in approval, and then he flew, and Pikka fought, and around them, the Nihil ships exploded, and somehow, impossibly, they survived.

***

"Those systems are linked to prevent overstressing the Longbeam's frame! You could have broken apart!" said another RDC flunky.

Joss rolled his eyes. He opened his mouth to answer, but Pikka got in first.

"Not with Joss at the helm," she said, simple, short, confident.

"I have a good feel for what a ship can take," Joss said.

Silence around the table, as the assemblage thought this over.

"So..." Admiral Kronara said, "you broke our ship to save our ship."

Joss nodded.

"Guess so."

The admiral looked at the chancellor.

"Thank you both," said the most powerful woman in the galaxy. "You may leave."

***

"*You may leave*," Joss said, perfectly imitating the chancellor's tone as he paced around their temporary quarters. "What the hell was that? We were doing them a favor fighting in that battle! We're not soldiers. We were just trying to help—from the *Legacy Run* disaster all the way to Kur, all we've done is try to help. And now they treat us like criminals!"

"It's all right," Pikka said. "It doesn't matter. It's over, and it doesn't seem like they're going to do anything to us for slicing the Longbeam."

"Pffff," Joss said. "Can't believe we got up early for this. Skipped breakfast! As a matter of fact..."

He stood up.

"Let's go eat. I'm starving, and you know how good the food is on Starlight. Let's hit a canteen, and then we'll find a transport back to Coruscant and take that little trip we've got planned, yeah?"

Pikka stretched and rubbed her eyes, trying to find a little energy.

"All right, Joss," she said. "I could use a cup of caf."

A chime from their door, and they both looked in that direction. Frowning, Joss tapped a control. The door opened, revealing Admiral Kronara.

"May I come in?" he said. "It won't take long."

"Are you going to throw us in the brig?" Joss said. "Fair warning, I don't do well in cages."

"I'm sure that's true," the admiral said. "No. I have an offer for you."

"Let him in, Joss," Pikka said, and her husband stepped aside.

The door slid closed behind Kronara, and he spoke.

"I'll make this simple," he said. "We are not confident that the Nihil we destroyed at Kur represented the entirety of their numbers. We have to be sure. Chancellor Soh has authorized the RDC to inaugurate a special task force to hunt down any Nihil that might be out there. Find their base, learn more, eradicate them if we can."

"Okay..." Pikka said.

"I would like you two to be part of that task force."

Joss snorted, incredulous.

"We're contractors," he said. "Spanner monkeys. What are you talking about?"

"You're innovative and brilliant. You two improvised strategies to save lives during the Legacy Run disaster, and then you figured out a way, on the fly, to survive completely new enemy tactics during the Battle of Kur. If you're willing, I could use you both. You seem to be the sort of people who like to help, and that's what I'm offering. The Republic needs you. Are you up for it?"

Pikka answered, without hesitation.

"No," she said.

Both Joss and the admiral looked at her, surprised.

"My husband and I had a vacation planned for when we finished our work building this station, and then we got caught up in all of this Nihil business, and it's been non-stop ever since. We deserve a break."

She folded her arms.

"So, we want our two weeks on Amfar. Sun, sand, and no fighting. But after that, I think we can do what you're asking."

"We can?" Joss said.

"Don't you think?" Pikka said, looking at him.

Joss considered.

"Yeah," he said. "I guess I do."

Admiral Kronara nodded, and stepped to the door.

"See you in two weeks," he said. "There's a lot to do."

The door closed behind the admiral, and Joss turned to Pikka.

"What do you think that means?" he said, seeming a little taken aback. "What did you sign us up for?"

She stepped up to him, reached her arms around him. Her hands barely met in the small of his back.

"I don't know, Joss," Pikka said, looking up at him. "But wherever we go," she smiled,"we'll go together."

THE END

First Duty

PART ONE

By Cavan Scott

Breathe, dammit. Breathe!

Velko Jahen was pleased that no one could hear the conversation that was running through her head as the shuttle dropped out of hyperspace.

The tall, silver-skinned Soikan had spent much of her life in the muddy trenches of her home planet, dodging blasters and evading remotes. She'd seen horrors that would stay with her forever, and bravery beyond compare, and here she was, a veteran of the Soikan conflict, dumbstruck by the sight of a gleaming space station.

Granted it was the most beautiful space station ever created, from its luminescent central disc to the majestic Jedi spire topped with the gleaming lantern that gave the facility its name: Starlight Beacon.

Velko had seen holos of Starlight, even studied the schematics, but had never realized how much the station looked like a gleaming lightsaber revolving regally in the star-filled expanse of the frontier.

"You're a long way from home, Vel," she said quietly to herself as the shuttle swept through the vast hangar doors. Of course, putting as many parsecs between her and Soika had largely been the point of applying to the Republic administration corps, to run from the ghosts of her past. No. That wasn't entirely true. She was here to serve the Republic, and where better than the symbol of light and hope on the fringes of the known galaxy?

That didn't stop Velko from being taken aback as the shuttle hatch opened. There were so many people. So much noise. She gripped hold of the ramp's safety rail, trying to center herself the way Dagni had shown her, although her surroundings couldn't have been more different from that of Soika battle command. The smell was better for a start, everything so new and lustrous. Her crisp Republic uniform was smarter than her old insurgent fatigues and her long white hair, usually pulled roughly into a ponytail, swept up immaculately into a tight triple bun that had taken her most of yesterday to master. And then there was the atmosphere. Not the air itself, although that was fresh enough; no, it was the sense of excitement that permeated the place, the feeling that anything was possible.

"Administrator Jahen!"

Velko turned at the sound of the voice. A green-skinned Ovissian was pushing through the throng, her smile almost as broad as the yellow horns that stretched from her head. "Welcome to Starlight. The Controller asked me to fetch you."

Velko felt herself straighten at Rodor Keen's title, a callback to her training. Even the Soika Liberation Force had respected the chain of command.

"Is the Controller in the operations hub?" Velko asked.

The Ovissian laughed, an infectious trill. "He wishes. He's in the medcenter."

Velko's eyes flicked down towards the scrubs her new companion was wearing, as pristine as the hangar's walls. "Is he well?"

"Oh, absolutely. The pressure hasn't got to him yet." The Ovissian's smile faltered for a moment. "That's not to suggest that he isn't up to the job. It's just... well, you'll see when we get there."

They hurried out into an equally packed corridor.

"I'm Okana, by the way."

"You're a medic."

"Junior nurse. Been here three days. Feels like three weeks."

"That bad?"

"Oh, no. Not at all. It's just been a lot." Okana's cheeks flushed emerald. "Sorry, I'm not putting you at ease, am I? My bedside manner isn't usually this bad, I promise."

Velko flashed what she hoped was a reassuring smile. "You're doing fine. I must admit, I'm feeling a little overwhelmed myself."

They slipped into a waiting turbolift, and the doors closed smoothly behind them. Okana jabbed a button and the car started up the shaft.

"Don't worry. That passes soon enough, or so I've been told..."

***

If the hangar bay had been awe-inspiring, *Starlight*'s medcenter was simply mind-blowing, especially for someone whose experience of medical facilities had been field hospitals caked with mud and the Force knew what else. Velko had never seen so many patients, even at the height of the insurgency. Okana led her through a seemingly endless succession of spotless wards, medical staff and droids flitting from one sufferer to the next. She spotted Amanin, Elomin, Boltrunians, and humans as they rushed past, even a couple of willowy Hassarians; one lying in a bone stabilizer and the other suspended in a bacta tank, an ammonia breather over its long snout.

"There are so many."

"Patients or wards?"

"Both." She couldn't help but be amazed at the medics, keeping calm in the face of such suffering. "Are these all from the Great Disaster?"

Okana nodded. "The Emergences? Yes. Can you imagine it? One minute you're living life as normal and the next debris is raining down from hyperspace. Hospitals are overrun from here to Vjun, if they exist at all. The worst cases are sent here, quite the operation by all accounts..."

The Ovissian led them through one last set of sliding doors, almost walking into two men Velko recognized from the briefing report she had been sent to read prior to her arrival. The Kessurian was Jedi Master Estalu Maru, resplendent in his temple robes, a squat orange and white astromech at his side. The human was who Velko had expected to welcome her in the hangar: Rodor Keen, head of Republic operations on Starlight and her direct superior.

"Controller," she said, extending a hand in greeting. "I'm Velko Jahen..."

"My new aide," Keen responded, and returned the gesture with a firm but not unfriendly grip. "I'm glad to finally meet you."

The implication in his comment took her by surprise. "I came as soon as I received the posting, sir."

Keen raised an apologetic palm "And I meant no offense, Administrator," he said. "Things have been a little hectic here, of late."

"Starlight is operating at peak efficiency," Maru protested. "I have been monitoring every department on a constant basis."

"With unwavering efficiency," Keen confirmed, the tension between the two men obvious. Velko could guess why. The station was co-managed by Republic officials and the Jedi Order, a symbol of the harmony between the two great institutions and, if their reputations were anything to go by, both Keen and Maru were known to be hands-on. You didn't have to be an empath to sense Keen's frustration as the Jedi continued, seemingly oblivious to the effect his words were having:

"Although, I have identified one-hundred-and-seventy-three improvements that could be made, from Cah Norne's engineering section to station security protocols."

"Improvements? This I have to hear."

All eyes turned to the Mon Calamari who stalked from a nearby room. Dressed in a security uniform, she moved like a caged targon, a holstered blaster hanging from her hip.

"Ah, Chief Tarpfen," Maru said, "I've been meaning to run through my recommendations with you. It shouldn't take long. Only an hour or two."

The Mon Cal crossed her muscular arms. "Is that all?"

"Administrator, may I introduce our Head of Security, Ghal Tarpfen. She's a new arrival, like you."

The Mon Calamari barely even acknowledged her, concentrating instead on Keen.

"Controller, this entire section is a diplomatic incident waiting to happen. We have patients from warring territories lying side-by-side, with no thought of what they might do to each other when they regain consciousness."

"Unfortunately, the Great Disaster paid little attention to political boundaries," Maru said, displaying a mastery of sarcasm that surprised Velko. "But that is why we are here, to ease any tensions that may arise."

Beside him, the astromech beeped with alarm.

"Kaysee-Seventyate is right, Maru. You and I have duties to perform elsewhere," Keen reminded the Kessurian before adding a hasty: "separately."

In response, Maru fished a datapad from his robes. "Nonsense. I can monitor operations as easily here as I could in the hub, and if Marshal Kriss requires me–"

"There is no need," Keen cut in, speaking before Tarpfen could cause a diplomatic incident of her own. "After all, we have Administrator Jahen..."

"Me?" Velko said, instantly wishing that her voice hadn't come out in such a squeak. "But I thought I would be working with you?"

Jedi's blade! Could she sound any more needy?

Keen was already walking for the door. "Don't worry, you'll be sick of the sight of me soon enough. The Chief will show you the ropes. Maru?"

The Jedi still wasn't showing any sign of following his Republic counterpart, not until KC-78 gave him a none-too-subtle nudge.

"Yes, yes, thank you my friend," the Jedi muttered as he allowed himself to be guided out of the ward. "I look forward to our little chat, Chief Tarpfen. May the Force be with you."

"I'll need it," the Mon Cal muttered, glowering at the back of the Kessurian.

"He's not what I expected," Velko ventured with a smile, only to be rewarded with a look cool enough to freeze lava.

"You're Soikan. A soldier?"

"Used to be."

"Part of the Livtak Union?"

"No. I fought for the Gagic Alliance."

Tarpfen frowned, studying the silver scales that lined Velko's sharp cheekbones and the lilac eyes she shared with the rest of the Jahen clan. "I'm sorry. I just thought, what with your coloring..."

"My father was Livtak, but my mother was Gagic."

"That must have been difficult."

"Not really. Father defected as soon as he realized what the Livtak were planning." Velko clapped her hands together, keen to change the subject. "So, where do you need me?"

She glanced around the ward, and was grateful for the warm smile she received from Okana. The junior nurse was assisting an Anacondan that Velko recognized from her files as Doctor Gino'le, the station's Chief of Medical Operations, a brilliant surgeon who had grafted cybernetic limbs to his snake-like body to better care for his patients. At present, he was administering drugs to a prone Medoslean, the huge jelly fish-like being spread over not one but two trauma-cots.

"You can start in there," Tarpfen said, thrusting a webbed thumb at the room behind her. "Good luck."

"With what?"

"You'll see."

The chief brushed past, heading for a cubicle on the opposite side of the ward, leaving Velko where she stood.

"Right. Excellent. I'll carry on then."

Chewing her lip, Velko turned and hurried into a room to find a craggy-faced Skembo lying on a medibed, both of his short legs in magna-casts. Beside him stood an impressive bodyguard droid, each of its four arms mounted with a blaster above a set of equally deadly-looking pincers.

"Who are you?" the Skembo demanded, with a voice like someone gargling rockrete.

"My name's Velko Jahen," she replied, still not knowing what she was supposed to be doing. She started towards the bed, only to stop sharp as the rocky-skinned patient squawked in alarm.

"You're supposed to wait by the door."

"By the door?"

"Yes. To guard it."

Velko shifted nervously, all-too-aware that the bodyguard was glaring at her with a single glowing photoreceptor. "I think there's been a mistake. I'm not a guard. I'll just go and find..."

"No!" the Skembo yelled, flicking out a long tongue to grab a grape from the bowl on the bedside unit. "I was promised a guard at all times and yet have been left alone for hours."

"You have your droid," Velko pointed out, wiping a grape pip he'd spat across the room from her cheek.

"But they made me drain his blaster gas! No weapons allowed on the ward, unless you're Starlight staff." His yellow eyes flicked down to her waist. "You do have a blaster don't you?"

Velko parted her hands in apology. "I'm afraid not. I'm just an aide, and–"

The Skembo didn't let her finish. "This is intolerable. Don't you know who I am?" At least he saved her further blushes of answering by providing the answer himself. "Ceeril? Ambassador of Rion?"

"Ah, yes, of course," she said, as if that explained everything.

"I was promised protection when I was brought here. There are Hassarians in the medcenter. I have seen them with my own eyes."

At least that made things clearer. The Hassarians and Skembo had been rivals for centuries, but neither of the lilac-maned Hassarians they'd passed earlier could be considered any kind of threat in their condition.

Velko was about to try to assuage the ambassador's fears when a crash sounded from the ward outside, followed by an ear-piercing siren.

"Now what's happening?" Ceeril yelped as Velko dived out of the door.

"I'll go see."

"No! Don't leave me," the ambassador screamed. "I'm not supposed to be left alone! What about the Hassarians?"

But the Hassarian menace, real or imaginary, was the least of Velko's worries. Ahead of her, the Medoslean had reared up from its repulsor bed, its fronds wrapped around the necks of both Okana and the serpentine surgeon. Tarpfen was already charging forward, her blaster unclipped.

"Don't shoot," Gino'le cried out before the security chief could fire. "She's having a reaction to the treatment. She doesn't know what she's doing."

"We need to stabilize her," Okana croaked, her voice almost unrecognizable as she pointed wildly at the floor.

Velko's eyes dropped down to a hypo lying just out of either medics' reach. "The injector—there!"

"I see it," Tarpfen said, diving for the booster as the massive patient convulsed. A tentacle shot out, striking the Mon Cal across the head. She flew back, her skull cracking sharply against a nearby medibed.

Velko didn't stop to check on the chief, even as Tarpfen slumped to the floor. A frond whipping out towards her, Velko raced forward, dropping beneath the tentacle to scoop up the injector as she slid past. Trying not to think about the awful rattle that was emanating from Okana's throat, she rolled back up and slammed the hypo into the Medoslean's crown, pressing down on the trigger. The booster gave a hiss and the Medoslean sagged, its rigid body deflating like a balloon, tentacles loosening from around the medics' necks.

"Thank you," Okana gasped, pulling herself free and looking over to Gino'le. "Are you alright, Doctor?"

"Quite well, Nurse," the serpent said, examining his patient, who was snoring lightly through her vocabulator.

Velko hurried over to Tarpfen who was attempting to use the end of the medibed to haul herself up.

"Woah there," she said, as the Mon Cal pitched forwards. "That was quite a knock."

"And quite a roll from you," Tarpfen acknowledged, grabbing hold of Velko's arms to steady herself. Velko allowed herself to enjoy the compliment as Doctor Gino'le scuttled over, metal legs clattering on the deck.

"Oh dear, dear, dear," he tutted, flashing a medical sensor into Tarpfen's eyes. "A level nine concussion if I'm not mistaken. You're going to need some time in a rejuvenator, Chief."

"Too much to do," Tarpfen slurred, attempting to stand on her own two feet with little success. "They're relying on me."

"Hey," Velko said, "I can look after things here. Even Ambassador Ceeril. Thanks for that, by the way. He's... quite special."

Tarpfen gave a punch-drunk but, Velko thought, genuine smile that dropped away as a scream rang out. Before any of them could stop her, the chief had pushed Gino'le aside and was staggering towards Ceeril's room where a Rodian patient was staring through the doorway, suckered hand over her mouth.

Tarpfen stumbled as she reached the threshold, but Velko caught her.

"Steady now."

"Don't waste time worrying about me. Worry about him."

Velko looked up and gasped. The ambassador's bodyguard was sprawled on the floor, a gaping hole where its head should be, but that wasn't the worst of it.

Ceeril himself was draped over the bed, head lolled back and mouth open, a column of twisting smoke rising from the blaster burn at the center of his chest.

TO BE CONTINUED...

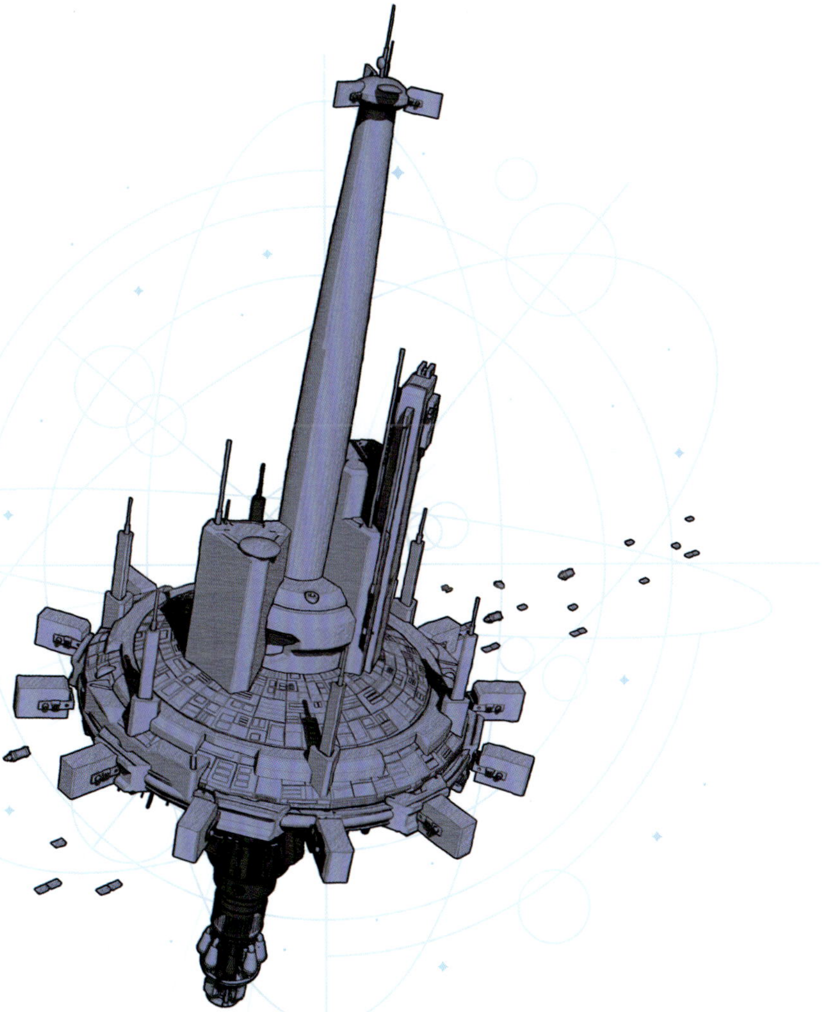

First Duty

PART TWO

By Cavan Scott

Everyone was talking at once, everyone except for Velko Jahen. The hours since the assassination attempt had been a blur. Velko could still see Ambassador Ceeril's body slumped back on the bed whenever she closed her eyes and was convinced that the smell of charred flesh still hung in the air, even here in Starlight Beacon's vast operation's hub. She had seen blaster wounds before, too many to remember, and they smelled much worse on the battlefields of Soika. Why had this attack, mounted not in the grime of a hastily dug trench but in the sterile medcenter of the Republic's newest and greatest space station, overwhelmed her?

"Administrator?"

It took Velko a minute to realize that Rodor Keen was talking to her. How many times had she forced Starlight's head of operations to repeat her rank before she responded. The look on his face provided the answer: too many!

"Sorry, sir," she stammered, annoyed at how flustered she sounded. "I was running through what happened one last time."

"An excellent idea," rang out a voice behind them. Velko and Keen turned to see one of the most striking figures she had ever seen striding towards them. Velko's heart sank. She had been waiting for this moment ever since she had received her posting, longing to meet this woman, but had never imagined it would be like this.

Jedi Master Avar Kriss, Marshal of Starlight Beacon and the Hero of Hetzal, was as impressive as you would expect from the person who had masterminded the Jedi response to the Great Disaster, saving billions of lives in the Hetzal system and beyond. Everything about her radiated confidence, from her flowing robes to the piercing blue eyes that were now set on Rodor Keen with the intensity of a targeting computer. Even the fact that she was flanked by a female Jedi at least three decades older than her, not to mention the towering Wookiee wearing Padawan robes, did nothing to diminish her presence in the room. Velko had the impression that Avar Kriss could be surrounded by every Jedi near and far, and all eyes would still rest on her.

This was not going to go well.

Beside them, Estala Maru took a step forward to greet the new arrivals in turn. "Marshal. Master Assek. Padawan Burryaga. Welcome back to Starlight. I trust your mission to the Malaga Cluster was a success?"

"The trade agreement between the Ayelina and Ludmere was signed without incident," Kriss confirmed. "And yet, we avoided one diplomatic crisis to find another raging back here on Starlight."

"Things have become a little heated in your absence."

"Which is something of an understatement," Keen interjected, a nerve throbbing in the temple above his cybernetic eye.

"What happened?" Kriss asked, turning her attention to the head of operations. "We could feel the disquiet the moment we arrived."

"Maybe you should see for yourself," Maru cut in before addressing the astromech that was never far from his side. "Kaysee, inform the medcenter that the Marshal is on her way."

***

Ceeril's room was exactly how Velko had last seen it, albeit more crowded with Kriss' party crammed around the now-empty bed.

"And this is where you found the Ambassador, Administrator Jahen?"

Velko nodded, her mouth dry. "Yes, Marshal. He was laid out on his back..."

"Having been shot in the chest."

"That's right."

"And what of his bodyguard?"

"Destroyed, its head blasted clean from its shoulders," said Ghal Tarpfen, Starlight's Mon Calamari head of security, who had been waiting for them in the ward. She stepped forward, pointing out tiny shards of metal embedded high in the far wall. "You can see shrapnel from its processors, here and here."

Standing by the door, Burryaga rumbled a question which Maru was quick to answer.

"The security footage is a mystery." The Kessurian nodded at his astromech who dutifully projected an image of the scene from earlier that morning. Velko frowned to see herself standing talking to Ceeril, the bodyguard droid still on its broad feet. Then came the commotion from outside, Velko diving from the door seconds before the image was lost with static. "The signal was scrambled minutes before the attack."

"The assassin covering their tracks," Nib Assek suggested as the astromech fast-forwarded until the image returned, the Skembo now prone on the bed and the droid toppling back with a crash.

"I still can't believe that nobody heard anything," Keen complained. "A blaster is hardly quiet."

"We were distracted," Velko admitted.

"With the incident with the... what was it again?" Assek asked.

"A Medoslean," Tarpfen told her. "The patient had a violent seizure and started attacking members of the staff, myself included. If it wasn't for Administrator Jahen here, the situation could have been much worse."

"Worse?" Keen snapped. "An ambassador has been shot on Starlight Beacon. Do you have any idea how many survivors we are caring for since the hyperspace disaster?"

"Eighteen thousand four hundred and seventy-four," Maru stated, drawing a furious glare from the coordinator. "Sorry. That was rhetorical, wasn't it?"

"Whatever the number," Keen continued, "Starlight is supposed to be a haven, a sanctuary, and yet this happened right under our noses."

"The real question is, what are you going to do about it?"

Jedi and Republic officials turned to see Ambassador Ceeril on the other side of the door. The rocky-faced Skembo was hunched in a repulsor chair, a bacta-vest covering his chest. Burryaga stepped aside to let Kriss pass, the marshal bowing in greeting to the injured official.

"Your Excellency, I am glad that you have survived your ordeal."

"No thanks to any of you," Ceeril wheezed, clutching his chest.

"That isn't entirely true," Maru pointed out, glancing up at nurse Okana who had pushed the ambassador back onto the ward. "If Doctor Gino'le and his staff hadn't responded so quickly..."

"The Hassarians would have got their way, yes I know."

"The Hassarians?" Kriss asked, drawing a glare from the pained ambassador.

"Those brutes won't rest until the Skembo are driven from the sector. Time and time again we've asked the Republic for help, and time and time again we've been refused."

"And you saw your assailant?"

"As clearly as I see you now."

"Unlike the cameras," Assek added.

"You found the hairs didn't you?" Ceeril asked, coughing harshly, "On my droid?" This was true. Velko had found them herself, hairs grasped between the droid's now-dormant pincers, the same color as those found in the manes of the Hassarians elsewhere in the infirmary. "How much evidence do you need?"

The ambassador's coughing intensified, his body wracked with agony. Doctor Gino'le scuttled over on mechanical legs, instructing Okana to push Ceeril to the room that had been prepared on the other side of the ward.The marshal's party watched him go, Rodor Keen's face as dark as the Skembo's had been pale.

Kriss turned to the coordinator as soon as Ceeril was out of earshot. "Do we have any Hassarians on the station?"

Velko spoke up before Keen could answer. "A couple, yes."

A scathing look from the coordinator shut her down again.

"And what do they have to say for themselves?" Kriss asked.

"Both were severely injured in the Wazta emergence," Keen said. "One has been in a bacta tank for three days and the other is barely conscious."

"Can we be certain about that?" Tarpfen asked.

"It would be the ideal cover," Assek agreed.

Kriss sighed. "Can I see them?"

"Of course," Tarpfen said, leading the group towards the next ward. "This way."

Velko went to follow, but was stopped by Keen. "Not you, Administrator."

Her brow furrowed. "Sir?"

"We need a full report for the Senate. Leave nothing out. Nothing at all."

So this was it. Velko was being sidelined, reduced to filing reports while Ghal Tarpfen led the way. So much for her glittering career on the Republic's first mega-beacon. She'd be shuffled into a corner of the ops hub before you could say "Dank Farrik."

It was only when she heard KC-78 burble that she realized that not all the party had left with Tarpfen. The astromech was still in the ward as was its master.

"I envy you," Maru told her, with the hint of a smile.

"You do?"

"A full report? All those juicy details? My kind of heaven."

She cocked an eyebrow. "You can write it if you want."

A wistful sigh escaped his thin lips. "Alas the station will not run itself. But I can imagine it, can't you Kaysee?" He glanced down at the little droid. "Evidence to collate from every witness. From the victim himself."

The astromech whistled shrilly.

"I stand corrected. Victims, plural. That unfortunate bodyguard."

"That destroyed bodyguard," Velko reminded him.

Maru regarded her with those curious scarlet eyes. "Of course. Now where did they take the poor thing?" He pulled a datapad from his sleeve and swiped the screen, the device rewarding him with a satisfying beep. "Ah, yes. In the security tower. Evidence room three."

Velko straightened where she stood, immediately picking up on the none-too-subtle hint Maru had just dangled in front of her. Perhaps there was more to this Kessurian after all.

"Do I have access to evidence room three?" she asked.

"No," the Jedi responded mischievously as he turned and swept from the room, "but Kaysee does..."

***

The security tower was as stark as the rest of the station was opulent, the walls a brushed gunmetal, the furniture sturdy but functional. The remains of the bodyguard droid were laid out on a raised slab, illuminated by lights that gave out a harsh blue light.

"Ready to record, Kaysee?" Velko asked the droid.

The astromech bleeped that it was.

"Okay. The bodyguard unit is intact except for the damage to its head." She glanced down at its mechanical hands. "The pincers have now been scanned to reveal traces of Hassarian DNA, confirming that the hair was from a Hassarian." She tried to imagine one of the tall creatures she had seen on the wards coming through the door, the bodyguard rushing forward to protect its master; a struggle, the droid ripping out a clump of hair. Something about it just wasn't right.

"Kaysee, can you replay the recording for me?"

KC-78's holo-projector whirred and Velko watched herself once again disappear through the door only to be replaced by static, the picture flicking back on to catch the bodyguard clattering to the floor.

"But where did the shot come from?" Velko wondered aloud.

KC bleeped a question, but she ignored him, leaning over to peer at the damage to the bodyguard's cylindrical head. Carefully, Velko ran a finger across the jagged edge where its single receptor unit had been, pulling free a scorched shard of metal.

"Can you scan this?" she asked her companion, holding the fragment in front of KC's microanalyzer. Blue light washed over the metal as processors buzzed and clicked inside the astromech's stubby frame.

"Well?"

The droid burbled excitedly as it delivered the verdict, and in an instant Velko knew who had shot the ambassador.

***

She could hear Ceeril complaining loudly as she approached his new room. Nib Assek and Burryaga had been posted at the door, an attempt to persuade the ambassador that the peril was being taken seriously. Assek nodded in greeting as Velko slipped into the room, KC-78 at her side, to find the Skembo berating Ghal Tarpfen as Okana attempted to change his dressings.

"I don't care what they're doing or who they've left to guard my room, I will not feel safe until Marshal Kriss or Coordinator Keen personally informs me what they are doing about the vile Hassarian threat. I demand justice. I demand action!"

"The threat has passed," Velko said, as calmly as she could, ignoring the puzzled glance the security chief gave her as she entered the room. "You are in no danger."

The Skembo's eyes widened. "You've deported the Hassarians from Starlight?"

Velko shook her head. "There is no need. Your 'assassin' is dead and gone."

What was left of the bodyguard's head clattered as she threw it onto his lap.

"What is the meaning of this?" Ceeril spluttered, pushing the decapitated unit away from him.

"I was wondering the same thing," Tarpfen said, pointing at the twisted hunk of metal. "That is evidence."

"It is," Velko agreed. "Evidence of a head blasted apart at pointblank range. We saw your poor bodyguard topple back and hit the floor the moment the cameras came back online. It did strike me as odd, however, that this same footage didn't show us the assassin."

"They must have fired from near the door," Ceeril stammered.

"Before running?"

"I wouldn't know. I was too busy clinging to life!"

"And yet, our mysterious assassin didn't fire when the droid was close enough to rip a clump of hair from their head. Instead, they waited until they'd almost escaped, shooting a bodyguard whose own weapons were deactivated." She pointed at the charred cranial unit lying in front of the horrified ambassador. "Weirdly, the head shows no evidence of blaster residue, although we did find traces of detonite inside the casing."

"*Inside*?" Tarpfen's question went unanswered as Ceeril flicked out an impossibly long and surprisingly sticky tongue that snatched the Mon Cal's blaster from her hip and pulled it back towards him.

"I don't think so!" the Mon Calamari snapped, grabbing the retreating tongue and holding it tight. The ambassador gagged and pulled back, but Tarpfen's grip held firm, the pair engaging in a bizarre tug-of-war.

"What is the meaning of this?" a voice bellowed as Rodor Keen appeared in the doorway, staring incredulously at the scene, Avar Kriss and an amused Estala Maru standing behind him.

"The Ambassador attempted to disarm me," Ghal Tarpfen told the controller, releasing her grip on the tongue, which snapped back into Ceeril's mouth with a sharp sluuck, the blaster clattering to the floor.

"Probably because he faked his own assassination," Velko said, nodding towards KC-78. The droid burbled in response and projected a holo of the bodyguard's remains spread out in the evidence room, with one slight difference.

"Is that a hidden compartment?" Keen asked, peering at a tiny hatch that lay open on the droid's chest.

"It is," Velko replied. "It took some finding, but when I did, Kaysee was able to detect Hassarian DNA within its chamber."

"The kind left when you stash false evidence in your own chest?" Tarpfen asked, glowering at the ambassador who was pressing the back of a cool hand against his throbbing tongue.

"As well as this," Velko said, producing a blaster gas canister from her pocket, "containing just enough eleton to charge a weapon. Enough to maim..."

"But not kill outright." Tarpfen looked as though she wanted to finish the job herself.

"It was daring," Velko admitted. "Programming your droid to fake the shooting, then detonate an explosive lodged within its cranial unit"

"Thus destroying any trace of the deception," Keen concluded, crossing his arms decisively.

"It's nonsense," the ambassador protested, shuffling back on his mattress, "that's what it is."

"Is that so?" Ceeril paled as Avar Kriss stepped into the center of the room, stopping at the foot of his bed. "Do you know how difficult it is to lie in front of a Jedi, Ambassador?"

"Especially as Administrator Jahen has supplied evidence in droves," Maru said, tapping his ever-present datapad. "All of which I have now sent to the Republic security service on Coruscant."

"Isn't that my job?" Ghal Tarpfen asked, sounding more amused than annoyed, her weapon back in her hand.

"That's the wonderful thing about Starlight Beacon," Avar Kriss said, turning back to Ceeril. "The Republic and Jedi working together for the good of all. I think we make quite a team, don't you, Ambassador? Perhaps it would be best if you spent the rest of you convalescence in the detention center."

"Do you want to do the honors?" Tarpfen asked Velko, but she shook her head. "You're the Head of Security."

"And you are owed a tour of Starlight," Rodor Keen told her as Burryaga maneuvered the Skembo's medibed out of the room, under Tarpfen's watchful gaze. "Tell me, where would you like to begin?"

The decision was taken out of her hands when a call came over the comm-system, a gruff, sibilant voice informing the Jedi marshal that they'd received a distress call from the Kazlin System.

"Maybe we should head to where the action is," Velko said as Avar Kriss led the way to the turbolift.

"An excellent idea, administrator," Keen agreed. "I think you're going to fit in perfectly."

THE END

Hidden Danger

PART ONE

By Justina Ireland

Velko Jahen and Ghal Tarpfen raced through the hallway outside Starlight Beacon's security hub to the nearest elevator, Ghal punching the button that would take them to the main concourse with a brutality that belied her inner distress.

"Do you think we'll make it in time to keep them from hurting each other?" Velko wondered aloud.

"We can only hope," Ghal said. As soon as the doors slid open, they charged out of the car and into a crush of bodies. As they forced their way through the baying mob, Velko struggled to figure out how things had turned so bad, so fast…

***

One Day Earlier

It was all wrong.

Velko looked at the banner hanging above the main bank of elevators that serviced the primary docking bays for Starlight Beacon and sighed. "Welcome Agricultural Alliance!" the strip of material proclaimed, the aurabesh characters stitched out in bright green letters against an ivory background.

"I thought we decided to go with blue," Velko said, frowning as she looked at her datapad for the banner order request.

"Blue? No, you wanted green," the creator of the banner, a Neimoidian who was well known for beautiful tapestries and draperies, scowled at Velko, evident displeasure radiating off him. "Controller Rodor Keen said green, for plants. Ergo, I give you a beautiful green banner."

"Not all plants are green," Velko muttered, but the banner was nicely constructed, stately and grand without being excessive. What did it matter that her meticulous plans had been changed by Rodor Keen once again? Sure, he might be the head of Republic operations responsible for Starlight Beacon, but couldn't he at least let her handle the decorations without any interference? Ah well, at least it hadn't been the Jedi Estala Maru this time.

"This is fine. What about the linens and such for the formal dinner?"

"All in order, my lady, all in order." The Neimoidian gestured toward the bank of elevators. "I can go and finish up hanging tapestries, yes?"

"Yes, yes, thank you." Velko said, only half paying attention as he waddled away to see to other tasks. She still had a dozen other small things to check before the delegates arrived, but most important was the security for the event, and that would require a visit to the administrative hub.

For the next few days, the Galactic Agricultural Alliance would be holding their annual meeting on Starlight Beacon. After the destruction in the Hetzal system, and the resulting upheaval with the hyperspace lanes, the annual meeting was the first big event Starlight would host, second only to its original inauguration. It would also be the first meeting of the agricultural alliance that welcomed members from all over the galaxy, and not just the few that usually made the trip to Coruscant, where it was usually held. With people from the frontier concerned about safety throughout the galaxy, especially with the Republic Fair rapidly approaching, the pressure to ensure that the event went off without a hitch was enormous. Who would have thought so many people would be so throroughly invested in keeping a bunch of scientists happy, Velko marveled? Not her, but on Thyrsus farming had been looked upon as an occupation undertaken only by those too cowardly to fight back. Over the past few days, however, Velko had been reminded that not every system found warfare more edifying than growing things, and now she was as determined as everyone else to make certain that this event was a success. That began with excellent security.

Velko made her way to the security office, opting to take the maintenance stairs rather than the elevator. She'd been lax in her fitness lately, and it seemed like a good way to also give herself a few moments alone to think. Too many now recognized her as the person on Starlight Beacon who got things done, or at least had a conduit to those who could, and she often found herself waylaid by someone wondering why there wasn't a certain dish being served in the dining lounge, or why the lights dimmed at a certain time, and numerous other minor grievances along the way. Some days it was hard to get anything done, especially when everyone seemingly forgot that living together on Starlight Beacon meant catering to the needs of lots of different species.

But she was getting much better at handling the demands and explaining to exasperated Republic officials and visitors just why she could not accommodate certain special requests.

After the first couple of flights of stairs Velko's thighs began to burn, and she started running, enjoying the feel of the muscles working in her legs. When she passed the doorway to the fifth floor, she found herself skidding to a stop as a brown-skinned human girl grunted under the weight of a giant pot of flowering vines.

There was nothing about the pot that should have alarmed Velko—it wasn't unusual to see the gardeners rearranging the plants that were tucked in various locations throughout the station—but there was something about these vines that reminded her of the Drengir. It was ridiculous, of course, as the plant in the pot wasn't eating the girl or trying to attack anyone, but everyone had been on edge since they'd had an infestation of the creatures on Starlight not so long ago, Velko being no exception.

"Hey, you shouldn't be back here," Velko gasped, more out of breath than she should have been after such a short climb. She really needed to start making time to exercise.

"Oh, my mentor told me that I was supposed to take these plants to the dining facility, and I had to do it within twenty minutes to ensure that the blooms didn't wither. This is a very fragile plant, and the ambient humidity in Starlight Beacon is approximately forty-five percent, which is far too low, but the garden up there is kept at eighty-five percent humidity, which is far more agreeable. Also, all the elevators were busy, and I was worried I wouldn't make it in time."

Velko blinked as the girl babbled on and held up a hand to interrupt her flow. "That doesn't really explain how you got back here?"

"Oh, I spliced the lock!" said the girl. "Republic standard locks tend to use a braided equivalency of the Gratton cipher, and the Maben algorithm set to a four-beat pulse. That's weird, right, that so many government locks throughout the galaxy respond to the exact same datapoints? Anyway, I don't have a lot of time to explain, but I'd be happy to show you later if you'd like."

Velko had the strange sensation she was falling from a great distance. "I'm sorry, who are you?" Velko crossed her arms as irritation spiked through her, and sniffed, aware of the spicy scent from the flowers in the pot the girl held. It tickled her nasal passages.

The door the girl stood before slid open, and a rose-gold childcare droid stood on the other side. "Well, Avon, looks like your calculations were incorrect because I did indeed beat you. I even went looking for you in the greenhouse, where this plant needs to be in the next eight minutes.And you owe me a jar of canuda oil for my joints."

"Avon Starros," the girl said with a toothy grin, ignoring the droid and answering Velko. "I'm here with the Galactic Agricultural Alliance for their upcoming symposium. I have to go, but I will make sure to use the elevators from now on!" the girl said, hefting the pot and hurrying after her droid, who kept up a steady chatter at the girl as the two left. Curious.

Velko exited the doorway immediately after the pair, but there was no sign of the girl or her droid.

Shrugging away the strange encounter, Velko turned her attention once more to preparing for the arrival of the rest of Agricultural Alliance.

***

A day later, after several rounds of arguments (or "vocal disagreements," as Rodor preferred to call them), everything was in place. Every fixture on Starlight seemed to have a little more sparkle, and sleeping quarters had been set aside and prepared for more than a hundred of the most important botanists, agricultural experts, and biologists in the galaxy. The food for so many extra bodies had been ordered and prepared, with extra care towards accommodating the particular likes and dislikes of each species. There were meats and vegetables for the carbon-based life forms, several soups and invigorating tinctures for the non-carbon-based life forms, and enough wine for a host of taverns. The scientists would be fed and well rested, and some of them possibly more than a little the worse for wear.

But that was entirely okay, because they had learned much about security after the instance with Ambassador Ceeril. There would be no surprises. Every long-standing treaty and disagreement had been considered.

Starlight Beacon was ready.

Velko stood in the docking bay and waited for the ships to start arriving. They had talked the Alliance into consolidating their travel so that the hundred or so scientists would be arriving in five ships: one from Coruscant, one from Chandrila, and three from each rim of the galaxy, specifically the planets Onderon, Ord Mantell, and Raxus. The scientists would be cranky and out of sorts after their trips, most people usually were, and Velko planned on greeting them and assigning them to their sleeping quarters quickly so that they could relax before the grand dinner later that evening.

Nothing would go wrong.

***

Hours later, after smiling and bowing and greeting one hundred and six agricultural scientists, Velko walked to the administrative hub to find Starlight's head of security, Chief Ghal Tarpfen, watching the monitors as they scrolled through different views of Starlight Beacon: the hangar bays, the dining facility, the meditation garden, the concourse, and on and on, the images scrolling past so quickly that they made Velko feel a bit dizzy.

"I'm amazed you can keep track of everything that's happening," Velko joked.

Tarpfen, a Mon Calamari with not a lick of humor, sipped at a cup of greenish liquid and said nothing for a long moment.

"Are you checking up on me? Because it's a bunch of scientists," she said, finally. "The most exciting thing they've done is walk through the meditation gardens sniffing the flowers. All of which are blooming—just as you wanted, by the way."

"Ah, I'll have to thank Castor for seeing to that." Velko had thought it would be nice to force the gardens into bloom for the scientists' visit, since they were all biologists and horticulturalists and the like. People who loved plants should love flowers, and it had seemed like a small ask of the gardener. Since Starlight's gardens were already on an artificial schedule it hadn't been a huge issue, but it was definitely nice to know they had managed to do it. Pretty flowers were low on the list of priorities when there were a hundred people to keep safe, fed, and housed, but it was a nice touch all the same.

A pinging noise caught Velko's attention, and she frowned at one of the bottom-most screens as it began to flash. "What's going on with that?"

Tarpfen leaned forward, putting her mug of tarine tea to the side. "It looks like a camera droid flagged an infraction in this area. The droids are programmed to recognize over three thousand different kinds of aggression responses."

"Aggression…?" Velko began, but she didn't get a chance to finish. On the screen, an Ithorian male lunged at an Amani, who responded by flipping their tail around and striking the Ithorian.

"Tarpfen!"

"On it," The Mon Calamari said, standing and following Velko as she ran out of the room.

***

The fight had been on the main concourse not far from the gardens, and by the time Velko and Tarpfen stepped out of an elevator nearby the Ithorian and the Amani were engaged in full-fledged combat. Neither uttered a word, instead they hissed and clicked at each other, their gutteral sounds both feral and vicious.

A crowd had gathered to watch the brawl, and getting through the throng was slow going. Tarpfen didn't hesitate. She pulled out her blaster and peeled off two shots aimed at the combatants, bringing them both down.

"Don't worry. I only stunned them," she exclaimed, in response to Velko's shocked expression.

"I know, but shooting our guests?" Velko shook her head. "That's never going to be a wise move." Still, the blaster fire had dispersed the crowd more quickly than yelling and pushing, but Velko was not impressed by Tarpfen's impulsive decision to fire on two beings in the middle of the concourse.

"You'd rather I'd let them pound each other into protein paste?" Chief Tarpfen asked, voice flat. Velko took a deep breath and sighed, but no sooner had she opened her mouth to tell the security droids to take the two brawlers to the medcenter than a stocky Siniteen with dull yellow skin and a frown of dismay interrupted her.

"What is the meaning of this?" the woman demanded, veins in the ridges of her large head throbbing with obvious displeasure. "How dare you start shooting at my colleagues so haphazardly?"

"These individuals were fighting," Tarpfen began, but Velko inserted herself between the two women and gave the Siniteen a small bow.

"My apologies, but Chief Tarpfen is correct. I am Administrator Velko, can I be of some assistance?"

"Ah, Velko, just the person I was looking for. I am Professor Sh'nar Qwasba, the current president of the Galactic Agricultural Alliance. I'm afraid I just arrived and did not get a chance to liaise with you earlier. I was of the mind that so far the hospitality on Starlight had been exceptional, but then I was told by my assistant that my colleagues were brawling on the concourse."

"Yes, which is why they were, um, subdued. We're going to have them taken to the medcenter."

"And then they will be detained until they understand Starlight Beacon has a zero-tolerance policy for fighting," Tarpfen interjected.

"It is somewhat extreme to be walking around shooting civilians, is it not?" Sh'nar said forcefully, her expression displeased. Velko agreed, Tarpfen should have shown more restraint, but either one of them might have killed the other had the chief not intervened.

"It was the best choice in the moment," the Mon Calamari said, blinking.

"Is that not what the security droids are for?" Sh'nar asked, crossing her arms.

"Droids aren't always best at assessing rapidly shifting situations, if you catch my drift," Chief Tarpfen said. "It was far better for your colleagues to take a stun bolt."

Medical droids and other personnel arrived on the scene to see to the injured fighters, including Okana, to whom Velko gave a small wave. The green Ovissian medic seemed to be very interested in the conversation between Chief Tarpfen and Professor Qwasba, but she turned her attention to the injured men as they were lifted onto medibeds.

"Professor, perhaps you would like to accompany us to the medcenter? Once the two offenders are checked out, we'll take their statements and release them into your care," Velko assured Sh'nar. "I'm sure that whatever brought them to blows was a minor disagreement, since you said they're old friends."

Before Velko could add anything, Chief Tarpfen held her hand up to the comm unit she wore strapped to her temple. Without a word, and little more than a nod at Velko, Tarpfen was running for the nearest elevator.

"And just where is she going?" asked Professor Qwasba, mystified. Velko didn't answer. She was hearing the same alert from Master Estala Maru in her earpiece.

"All Jedi and security details, report to the dining facility immediately. Riot in progress. This is an emergency."

Velko's stomach tightened in fear as she hurried after Tarpfen, remembering the girl who'd been carrying strange vines to that facility. Vines that had reminded her of... the Drengir!

TO BE CONTINUED...

Hidden Danger

PART TWO

By Justina Ireland

Velko Jahen, administrator of Starlight Beacon, ran down the concourse after Ghal Tarpfen, Starlight's head of security, the Mon Calamari setting a brutal pace.

"All units, I repeat, all units, please respond to the dining hall. There is a riot in progress." The voice in Velko's comm piece, Jedi Master Estala Maru, remained calm and unbothered. That was okay, as Velko was upset enough for the both of them.

Velko burst into the dining facility a few seconds after Ghal, only to slide to a stop. When Master Maru had said "riot," Velko hadn't really understood what he'd meant by that. She'd expected to find people smashing displays and ransacking things. But the scene before her was less of a riot and more a brawl: a Devaronian woman punched a Czerialan man before being tackled from behind by a human. A Mirialan in a hoverchair yelled in rage before speeding toward a hapless Ugnaught who managed to dive out of the way moments before being hit, the hoverchair smashing into the wall instead.

Everywhere in the room people were fighting. And not just any people—these were the scientists who had gathered on Starlight Beacon for the Galactic Agricultural Alliance conference.

"Still feeling it's maybe 'rude' to shoot our guests?" Ghal asked drily. Not moments before they'd had to stop a brawl on the main concourse, and Velko had been horrified by Ghal shooting the combatants. Not with a full-powered blaster bolt but a stun bolt designed for just such things. It had been, in hindsight, a quick way to pry order from chaos.

"No, I think perhaps it's our best option. Unless you have other ideas?"

"Perhaps we can be of some assistance?" said a gentle voice.

Velko turned to find half a dozen Jedi standing behind her. There were few she recognized, but no surprise there. The Jedi were always coming and going, and trying to keep track of all of them on Starlight at any given time was like trying to count stars while in hyperspace.

"Administrator Velko," said the closest one, stepping forward. She recognized the dark-skinned human: Gil Jaretto, a Jedi Master visiting from Dubraib, a watery planet on the frontier. "Perhaps it would be best to let us handle this matter?"

"As long as you can restrain the scientists without anyone getting injured," Velko said. Gil bowed his head in respect and the knot of Jedi stepped forward, hands raised toward the group in the dining facility. For a moment the melee beyond continued before everyone froze, expressions slack.

"Oh, thank the stars—" Velko began, before the fighting broke out once again, the Jedi frowning with effort as they tried to calm the combatants beyond.

Ghal made a noise of derision and shrugged. "I think that ship has left the docking bay," she said, gesturing to the full-scale brawl just beyond the threshold. "But no, Jedi, this is something we can handle. Ateseven!"

A security droid, one that had appeared as the Jedi were responding, lumbered forward.

"Deploy non-lethal crowd suppression," Ghal ordered.

"Deploying crowd suppression," the droid replied. A spigot extended from its chest, foam spewing out in an arc as it trundled into the dining facility. "Thirty seconds until full suppression."

"Cut off air filtration to the dining hall," Ghal ordered into her communications earpiece. To the group crowding the doorway she said, "We need to take a step back."

Velko caught a glimpse of the foam expanding to fill the place, a floral scent tickling her nose before the doors slid closed. She smiled tightly at the Jedi, who nodded in acknowledgement, an awkward silence hanging over the group until the right time had elapsed.

The doors slid back open, revealing nearly a hundred agricultural scientists of different species completely covered in foam and sleeping soundly.

"Master Gil, thank you so much for your help. Would you and the rest of the Jedi mind patrolling the hallways to make sure there are no other violent outbreaks? Ghal and I can oversee this with the med team," Velko murmured, ignoring the look of triumph the Mon Cal sent her.

"Absolutely, Administrator Jahen." The Jedi walked away, and Velko sighed.

"We need to get every one of these people examined. This isn't how civilized scientists behave. Something caused this. Something deliberate."

"You don't think an entire contingent of scientists devolved into a slugfest over the proper way to irrigate a crop of khema?" Ghal muttered sarcastically.

"No," Velko replied. "And we need to find out what it was before someone gets themselves killed."

***

"I have taken samples from about half of the combatants," stated Doctor Gino'le, the Anacondan in charge of the medcenter, his prosthetic metal arms waving around in agitation. "Every reading is completely normal."

"Nothing unusual?" Ghal asked. "That seems odd."

Having suspected some kind of toxin, airborne or imbibed through food or liquid, Ghal had dispatched med teams to run sensor sweeps on the shuttles the scientists had arrived on, the quarters they'd been given, everywhere that members of the Agricultural Alliance had congregated, but nothing had been found, save for the soporific compounds left over from the foam the security droid had dispersed.

"I can only surmise that whatever they were exposed to, if indeed they were, has a very short half-life, breaking down quickly in the circulatory system. Even some of my patients with slower metabolisms have returned normal readings. So, I'm afraid I do not have a good explanation for you."

"Frustrating," Ghal growled.

Doctor Gino'le gave Ghal a smile. "The good news is that the two you stunned are now awake. You can question them, if you would like."

The Ithorian and the Amani were resting in separate wards of the medcenter, kept apart just in case of further violence, restraining straps securing them to their beds. Velko and Ghal didn't have time to waste, so they split up—Velko talking to the Amani while Ghal spoke with the Ithorian. If the aggression spread across the entire station, there was no telling what might happen. Velko had lived most of her life fighting an endless war, and she knew how quickly the peace could break. She wouldn't let mayhem reign on Starlight.

"What happened to me? Why am I restrained?" the Amani croaked as Velko entered the room, the green-yellow skin of his body glistening with slime, his long arms and overly large hands both secured at his side. The tip of his tail twitched in irritation.

"You were in a fight," Velko said. "Don't you remember?"

"I remember naught," The Amani replied, confused.

"I'm Administrator Velko Jahen. I work here on Starlight, and I am in charge of overseeing the agricultural conference. Maybe we can figure out what happened to you?"

"That would be ideal, Administrator. I am Doctor Prot Xan, a biologist from Hyko Academy on Hosnian Prime. This is highly unusual."

"I agree," Velko said, giving the Amani a smile in the hope it would diffuse the tension already creeping into their conversation. "Can you tell me what you remember?"

"Yomo and I had secured our lodgings and were on the way to dinner when we decided to take a tour through the gardens, off the main concourse. We were walking, and then Yomo said something… I'm not sure what, to be honest. I just felt annoyed, and then angry, and the next thing I remember I woke up here."

"Which gardens were you in? Was it the exhibition gardens or the meditation garden? Do you remember seeing any Jedi?" Both were impressive, but only two of many, the plants supplementing the atmosphere scrubbers in keeping Starlight's air fresh. The Jedi tended to frequent the quieter meditation garden.

"No Jedi, but I do remember something. Yomo wanted to find the submission from Professor Glenna Kip, a hybrid version of johta, one that was supposed to be hardier and easier to cultivate, especially created for arid climates. I believe we found it, although now I am uncertain. There was a flower, on a series of vines, with a scent that reminded me of home and the hunts." Doctor Xan leaned back, closing his eyes, and breathing evenly. "Ahhh, what a wonderful time that was."

Doctor Xan straightened, the Amani's beady black eyes suddenly alert. "You said I was in a fight? Who was the other combatant?"

"An Ithorian. I believe it was your friend, Yomo?"

"*Yomo*? Oh dear! Yes, Yomo is an Ithorian, but he is my oldest friend. We went to university together. He was the one who convinced me to turn my molecular biology focus to agricultural. Oh dear, oh dear. This is simply out of character for Yomo! He's a brilliant scientist, but a fighter he is not."

Velko asked the doctor a few more questions, but learned nothing conclusive, his distress overshadowing his answers. Trying not to let her frustration show, she thanked the Amani and made her way to the medcenter lobby, where she found Ghal waiting.

"Well, that was a waste of time," Ghal said with a burbling sound that Velko took as the Mon Calamari equivalent of a sigh.

"Maybe not. Did Doctor Yomo remember anything beyond the flowering vines and a visit to the gardens?"

Ghal shook her head. "No, which is useless. A plant? How could a plant cause all of this?"

"I'm not sure, but perhaps there's something on the plant. A stowaway, so to speak. There was a human girl with a strange plant. I think it might be somehow involved."

Ghal shrugged. "Perhaps. Let's go check it out."

Ghal and Velko walked through three different gardens before they found the flowering vines that Doctor Xan had mentioned. They had wrapped themselves around several of the surrounding trees and plants and seemed out of place, even though Velko recognized them.

"Just as I thought. We need to find the girl who brought that plant in yesterday. I saw her in the maintenance stairway."

"Have you been slacking on your fitness regime again?" Ghal asked, and Velko shrugged.

"I've been busy."

Ghal studied the twisting vines pensively. "I'm no expert on surface plants, but isn't that quite a bit of growth in just a few hours?"

"An unprecedented amount of growth. I would be worried that this was a Drengir, but the fact that we've been standing here for a few minutes and it hasn't tried to eat us puts that idea to rest." Velko cautiously stepped closer to one of the vines. It didn't writhe, not like the Drengir she'd seen, but it did seem active.

"Careful," Ghal called, seemingly from far away.

A woodsy citrus scent tickled Velko's nose. She blinked once, and again. The plant before her shifted and transformed, suddenly taking on a monstrous shape.

"Drengir!" she gasped, reaching for her blaster. But the weapon was gone, nothing at her side at all.

Another blink and Velko was no longer on Starlight Beacon. Instead, she was back on Soika, her platoon advancing on some hill defenses while blaster fire rained down all around her.

"Velko! Stop standing there and take the blasted hill so we can knock out that heavy cannon."

Velko turned to see Adjutant Captain Aila Gris yelling at her just before a blaster bolt found its mark. Aila was thrown back a meter, dead before her body hit the ground.

"*No, no, no.*" Velko panicked, pulling at her hair. How was she back here? Hadn't she done everything she could to get as far away from this place as possible? She had to get out of here, and like so many other bad memories on Thyrsus, the only way out was through.

Velko landed a fist in the nearest combatant. But the man didn't go down. Instead, he roared and dove at her. Velko crouched, ready for the attack. She would kill anyone who stood in her way.

The man charged forward, but when she kicked out at him he caught her foot and spun her around, throwing her into a column. Velko stood, angry and confused. Why was there a column on the battlefield?

The man dissolved, and just as quickly as she had fallen into the nightmare, Velko found herself back in the gardens. Ghal stood nearby, gingerly checking her jaw wasn't broken, her usually annoyed expression somehow bemused.

"Impressive, Administrator Jahen. I didn't think you had it in you."

Velko blinked again. A voice, Rodor Keen maybe, said, "She's still a bit confused. Can you hit her once more?"

A mist fell over Velko, cool and calming. And her confusion drained away. "I'm on Starlight?"

"You are." Rodor Keen stepped forward, a kind smile on his face. Behind Rodor stood a strange woman, her green skin laced through with silver lines. There was a vague reptilian look to her, and her head was wrapped with a turban, her lab coat splattered with a host of multihued compounds.

"What happened? One moment I was fighting a Drengir, and then I was back on Soika..." Velko trailed off, her head pounding. "Was that all in my head?"

"A hallucination, I'm afraid. Caused by the johto bloom. Apologies, it wasn't supposed to bloom here, I was still working on that, ah, less desirable property." The strange woman said.

Rodor cleared his throat. "Velko, this is Professor Glenna Kip. She's the scientist who created this hybrid. The aggression we've been experiencing is a side effect of her splicing the johto flower with a less violent strain of the Drengir."

"Are you serious?" Velko demanded, her rage rising once more, this time with an actual target.

"That's what I said," Ghal muttered, shooting the professor a murderous look.

"The Drengir's return reminded me of a similar project I had once undertaken, although last time I will say the outcome was not so... fertile," the professor attempted a smile. "The Republic thinks the hardiness exhibited by the Drengir could be useful in growing crops on some of the less fertile planets on the frontier. Not to mention the value of knowing more about the Drengir in case there are future challenges."

"We had a riot in the dining hall," Velko said, voice flat.

"Yes, and my apologies for that," Professor Kip said with a slight bow. "Avon?"

The small human girl with the deep brown skin that Velko recognized from seemingly a lifetime ago ran over.

"Avon, do you still have that salt block I gave you?"

"Yes, Professor Kip," the girl said with a smile, producing it from her pocket. Kip buried the salt in the pot, and immediately the flowers began to wither and die. In less than a minute the whole plant had withered, leaving behind nothing but a dead leaves and brown twigs.

"Johto is incredibly difficult to grow beyond the atmosphere of its home planet, and salt has an immediate effect on it. I've given the component list of the neutralizing compound to your environmental engineers, so there should be no further ill effects from the blossoms."

Velko couldn't agree with the professor. She still felt shaky and out of sorts from reliving the memory of the assault on Qunatos. It would be some time before she would feel anything close to normal.

"If you spliced Drengir plant material with an existing crop, what's to stop others from doing the same?" Ghal demanded. "It's hard enough when they infect the living, now we have to worry about them seeding themselves?"

"Oh no, that won't happen," Professor Kip said with a dismissive wave. "I've tried creating seeds from the Drengir, and it has proven utterly impossible. They cannot be seeded anywhere. Limiting their spread is one of the things the Alliance has gathered to discuss, and our data indicates that they never, ever seed themselves."

Velko wasn't convinced, but she had a pounding headache and the last place she wanted to be was anywhere near plants, or experts on them.

Ghal clapped a heavy hand on Velko's shoulder. "Come on. You look like you could do with a drink, and I'm not talking tarine tea."

"What about the Galactic Agricultural Alliance?" Rodor called after Ghal and Velko as they walked away. "They've barely gotten settled in!"

"I'll tell Professor Qwasa to find you if she has any questions," Velko replied.

"I really want you to show me that punch again, when you're up to it," Ghal confided.

Velko winced "I'm really very sorry about that," she said.

"Don't be," Ghal laughed, a strange chuffing sound from her throat. "It's the first time I've liked you."

THE END

Past Mistakes

PART ONE

By Cavan Scott

Velko Jahen let out a long breath as she closed the channel to Starlight Beacon's main control hub. She had just overseen yet another deployment of Jedi Vectors, the third of the day, the sleek fighters encased in the triangular hyperframes that would allow them to make the jump to lightspeed. The drift, commanded by Frozian Jedi Nooranbakarakana, was speeding to assist Marshal Kriss, who was currently engaged in a battle with Nihil raiders in the Magaveene system.**

Life hadn't exactly been quiet since Velko's posting to the Beacon, but the last few months had bordered on mayhem. Operation: Counterstrike was the official response to the atrocity on Valo, where the Nihil had razed the Republic Fair to the ground. Starlight was in the thick of the action, the launchpad of dozens of missions to flush the Nihil out wherever they were hiding. Velko's days—as well as most of her nights—were now spent coordinating various attacks, largely acting as a liaison between the Jedi and assorted Republic Defense Coalition forces. She'd thrived at first, the heightened emotions on the station reminding her of her previous life in the trenches of Soika, but now the adrenalin was starting to run thin. Now she was tired to her bones.

Velko checked her chrono. It would be another four hours until she could collapse in a heap on her bunk. Perhaps she could grab a quick caf from the concourse before the next crisis hit.

The trill of her comlink told her that wasn't going to happen.

"Jahen here," she said, trying to keep the weariness from her voice as she answered the call.

"Administrator, are you busy?"

Velko tried not to sigh audibly at the sound of Ghal Tarpfen, the Beacon's Head of Republic Security. What a question to open with. Who wasn't busy these days?

"What do you need, Chief?"

"There's a... fracas happening in Hangar Bay Four."

"A '*fracas*?'"

"Can you swing by? Like, now?"

Velko pinched the bridge of her nose. A headache was forming behind her eyes.

"Can't anyone–"

The Mon Cal didn't let her finish. "I'd go, but I'm processing Nihil prisoners brought in by Firebird Squadron."

"How's that going?"

"Good," Tarpfen replied. "I'm only two dozen behind schedule, which is better than yesterday. The last thing I need is to hotfoot it all the way over to bay four..."

"When I'm in the next section."

"You got it. I would say please but--"

Velko couldn't help but smile. "But it gives you a rash."

"That and grilled ormachek. So can you?"

Velko's relationship with Ghal had been rocky at first, but the two had become closer of late, thrown together by the crisis following Valo. She wouldn't say they were friends yet, but they were heading in that direction.

"I'm on my way," she said, making for the doors. "But you owe me one."

***

Oh, how Tarpfen owed her...

The 'fracas' turned out to be an argument between a visiting spacer and a very particular Trandoshan. Jedi were supposed to be calm and controlled at all times, but there was no mistaking the outrage on Master Sskeer's green face. When Velko saw him, the hulking Trandoshan was ripping the lids off packing crates with his sole arm, the other—although now growing back—having been lost in battle before Velko arrived on Starlight. Sskeer was known to be a force to be reckoned with at the best of times, but the situation was made oh-so-much worse by the fact that Velko recognized not just the ship the Trandoshan was standing in front of, but the trader he was arguing with.

"Vane?"

The last time she had seen Vane Sarpo, the Vuman had been covered in mud from the battlefields of Soikan, a 599-repeating blaster in his hands and a gash bleeding heavily above his left eye. Now only a ghost of a scar remained on his forehead, and his filthy combat fatigues were replaced by a luxurious silk shirt that perfectly matched the color of the electric blue tattoos that covered his face, the elaborate pattern of lines and symbols having grown considerably since they'd last met.

"Velko!" Vane exclaimed, his dark eyes lighting up when he saw her. "Velko Jahen. What in Vuma's name are you doing here?"

"I thought the uniform would be a clue," she said, crossing her arms.

"It certainly suits you," he said, looking her up and down. The old Sarpo charisma was still there, although many—including Dagni, Velko's closest confidante back in the Liberation Force—had considered it rather more smarm than charm.

"You know this... individual?" Sskeer hissed, his voice even more sibilant than usual.

"Of course," Vane cut in with a cheeky grin before she could answer. "We're old—"

"Friends," Velko cut in quickly not knowing what secrets Vane was about to spill in front of the Jedi.

Vane pursed his lips. "More than that, I'd say."

"We fought together," she explained, ignoring him. "During the civil war on my homeworld."

Sskeer appraised the Vuman with distrust. "He is not Soikan."

"And you are a very observant man... I mean, lizard... I mean... what do I call you?"

"Jedi," came the rumbled reply.

Vane chuckled, utterly oblivious to either Sskeer's frustration or Velko's mortification. "I suppose I used to be a... soldier of fortune."

Sskeer's lip curled to show a row of sharp teeth. "A mercenary."

"But not anymore," Vane told him. "Now I am a humble trader, along with Clune over there." He nodded to a nervous-looking Peasle who was trying her best to seal the crates that Sskeer had been investigating. Velko couldn't blame the little insectoid for being skittish. Peasles were timid beings at the best of times, liable to roll up into a ball at the first sign of trouble. A disgruntled Jedi Master definitely counted as trouble.

"What are these?" Velko said, reaching into the nearest crate and extracting a small plastic statuette.

"They are an insult," Sskeer informed her, looking as if he couldn't decide whether to crush the offending item or boot it out of the nearest airlock.

"They're art," Vane said, going to remove the statue from Velko's grasp. She pulled it away sharply, turning it over in her hands. The figure was of a woman with long blonde hair holding aloft a glowing sword, robes billowing behind her in the most melodramatic way possible.

"Is that supposed to be—?"

"Jedi Master Avar Kriss," Vane said proudly. "The Hero of Hetzal herself. Aren't they great? I picked them up from the most talented Snivvian sculptor on Cadomai Prime. Seriously, the guy's a genius. Just look at these?"

He rummaged in the crate and produced a model of a spacecraft that was both familiar and almost comically wrong.

"A Jedi Vector?" Velko said.

"Absolutely."

"A Jedi Vector with six wings."

Vane frowned at his merchandise. "How many are they supposed to have?"

"It doesn't matter if they have four, six, or seven hundred," Sskeer growled. "They are not being sold on this station."

"But why?" Vane asked, throwing his arms wide to take in the entire bay. "Look at this place. People come here from all over the Outer Rim, and why?"

"For help," the Transdoshan told him.

"Wrong." Sarpo actually went so far as to prod Sskeer in the middle of his barrel chest. "To see you all. To see the Jedi! And what better than to take a souvenir of their trip away with them. In fact, I'm sure my snaggletoothed friend could whip up a quick statue of you. Folk would go crazy for that. Seriously, they would fly off the shelves."

Velko's heart sank even lower as Vane glanced at Sskeer's armored stump. "Should I get him to do one arm or two?"

Stars alive! What was he thinking?

Velko stepped in between them as the Trandoshan took a dangerous step towards the trader. "Master Sskeer. Let me deal with this."

The Jedi actually growled, deep in his throat. "I don't want to see those things in any of the shops on any of the concourses. They are not to be sold on Starlight or anywhere else."

"Fine," Vane said behind her. "I get it. No statues." There was a pause and a rustle and Velko really didn't want to turn around. "But what about a souvenir mug?"

***

"'What about a souvenir mug?'"

Velko looked down at the cheap ceramic receptacle on the table in front of her, the lopsided graphic of Starlight Beacon printed upside down.

Vane took a sip of his ale. "It was worth a try. What is it with that guy anyway? I thought Jedi were supposed to be all one with the universe." Vane illustrated his point by wiggling his long fingers in front of his face. "I thought he was going to rip my arms off."

"The least you mention arms, the better," Velko said pointedly, rubbing the back of her neck. "Sskeer is... a special case. Under all that bluster he's..."

"Yes?"

She shook her head, looking up at the domed ceiling. "Actually I have no idea. Cantankerous? Surly?"

"A pain in the—?"

"Another drink?" Velko jumped at the sudden interruption from the waitress droid who had hovered up to them.

"Not for me." she said, before quickly adding: "And not for him either. We're not staying."

Vane blew out air as the waitress continued to the next table. "Spoilsport."

"You're lucky I didn't order you off the station immediately."

"And miss the pleasure of my company?" Vane gave her his best smile. The same smile that had got her into all kinds of trouble in the past. "You wouldn't do that, not after all this time."

She tried not to grin back. It was good to see him, and even better to get off her feet, taking the break that she had been promising herself for at least three work cycles. They'd come to Unity, Velko's favorite tapbar on the station, a bustling watering hole at the foot of the merchant's tower. Nurse Okana had introduced her to the place not long after Velko had first arrived, and it was a good alternative to the bars frequented by Republic staff, meaning they could relax without being bothered about work. At least that was the idea. It had been weeks since Velko first tasted what had swiftly become her favorite drink, a Teralov Thruster garnished with fresh olap from the station's bio-gardens, an admittedly flamboyant drink that Vane was now regarding with some amusement.

"What would your squad say if they saw you with that?"

Velko took another sip. "They'd probably charge me for desertion. Only gagic rum for Soikan's finest."

The way he was looking at her made her flush all over again. "You happy here, Vel?"

She nodded. "Of course."

"You look tired."

"And you look more colorful than ever," she said, pointing at the blue lines on his face. "I thought you weren't getting any more tattoos."

His smile faltered for a second as he rubbed his patterned cheek. "You know me. I always like to stand out in a crowd." She was about to ask if he was okay, when he steered the conversation back to her. "I'm just surprised to see you here of all places. Wearing that uniform, playing diplomat with Jedi."

"I'm doing a lot more than that."

"I don't doubt it, but… after everything we went through on the fields of Dionas, don't you want to see the galaxy rather than being holed up in one place?"

At first Velko didn't know what to say, but once she started to answer the words didn't stop coming. "This feels like it matters you know, the work we're doing here, especially since Valo. People are looking to Starlight for help, not just because of the Jedi, but because we offer certainty in an increasingly uncertain galaxy. You know what it's like out there at the moment, Vane. People are scared, really scared, for the first time in years."

"I get that, but why you, Velko? Is this really what you want to—"

He cut off sharply, wincing in pain, his hand going to his forehead.

"Vane?"

He forced an embarrassed smile. "Sorry…" he said, rubbing his temple. "Headache. Must be the light in here. It's been a while since I've been in a place like this…"

Velko frowned. She could always tell when Vane wasn't telling the truth… or when he was distracted. As he spoke, his gaze flicked over her shoulder, looking intently at something—or someone— behind her.

She turned to see a stunning female Zeltron sitting at the bar next to a massive Houk who was only slightly less imposing than Sskeer. The Zeltron was looking back.

Velko put down her drink, shaking her head. How could she have been so stupid? Vane's wardrobe had changed but his habits obviously hadn't... or his wandering eyes. Once a player, always a player.

She stood, straightening her tunic with a sharp tug. "I should have left you to Sskeer. I'd clear out if I were you."

His attention snapped back to her. "Sorry?"

"Your ship..."

"The *Rapscallion's Heart*."

"I think you'll find the docking permit has just elapsed."

"You're joking?"

"It should only take you thirty minutes to disembark. Twenty if you hurry."

"What? Wait... Vel!"

But Velko was already walking. "That's Administrator Jahen." she snapped as Unity's doors slid open and she stormed out.

***

It took Velko most of the twenty minutes she'd given Vane to calm down, and then only a couple of seconds for the shame to sink in. What had she been thinking? Revoking the man's docking privileges because he was making eyes at a pretty Zeltron? Vane had always been one for the ladies, even back when they were on the front line. She hadn't minded then. Liked it even. The last thing she'd needed was a relationship in the middle of a warzone, so their casual, no-strings-attached whatever-it-was-they-had suited her fine. So why react so badly now? She must have been more exhausted than she thought.

Thankfully the logs showed that the *Rapscallion's Heart* hadn't departed yet. The least she could do was apologize. But when she arrived back in Hangar Bay Four Vane Sarpo wasn't alone. She'd half-expected to find the Zeltron with him, but not the Houk who was peering into one of the crates. That was until he spotted Velko making her way through the docked ships, and slammed the lid shut, the sudden noise shocking Clune so much she immediately curled into a ball.

"Velko!" Vane exclaimed, a little too loud, raising his hands as if to ward her off. "I'm leaving. I promise. I just..."

His words trailed off and Velko felt a tug in her stomach, an instinct she had learned to trust not just about Vane, but anyone who wasn't telling the truth.

"Open the crate," she commanded brusquely.

"There's no need," Vane said. "My friend here was just looking to see if he wanted to take any of the merch off my hands, but as your pal Sskeer pointed out, they're rubbish."

"Yeah," the Houk muttered, making to hurry off. "Load of old tat."

Something wasn't right. Velko lunged at the nearest crate, yanking off the lid.

"Vel, don't!"

Now the Houk was all but running, but for what reason? A crate of tacky Jedi merchandise? That didn't make any sense... unless...

Velko reached into the case, grabbing hold of the top tray of statuettes. It came away easily, revealing more knickknacks below. She threw the tray aside, the plastic ornaments clattering on the deck as she reached for the next layer. This time Vane

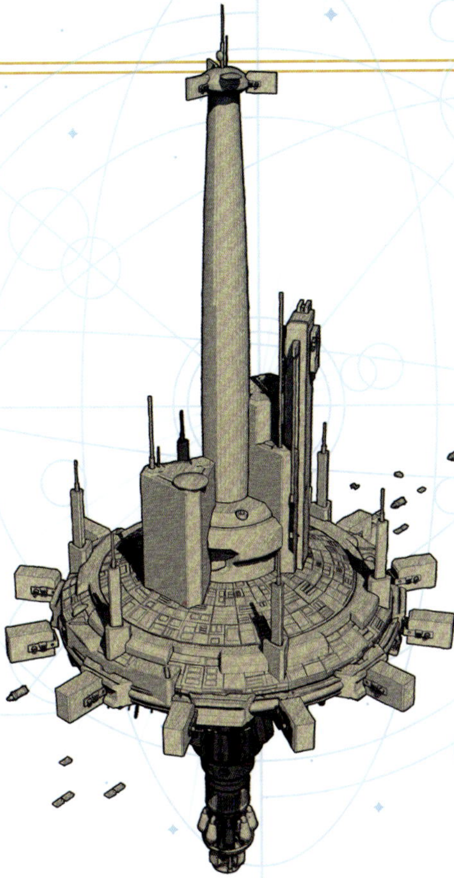

didn't try to stop her. Instead he scooped up Clune and raced for the *Rapscallion*'s ramp, Velko gasping when she saw what was hiding beneath the souvenirs.

"Vane! Stop right there!"

Vane didn't listen, as he went charging up the ramp. With a grunt of exertion, Velko threw the tray, cheap statuettes flying everywhere as it landed at Vane's feet. The Vuman stumbled, Clune rolling from his hands as he fell. Velko was on him in an instant, twisting his arm so he couldn't escape.

"What have you done?" she hissed as he struggled.

"More than any of us expected," hissed a voice from behind.

It was Sskeer, lightsaber burning as he led the now-cuffed Houk back towards them, Ghal Tarpfen at his side.

"Sskeer did some digging," the Mon Cal said as Velko pulled Vane back to his feet. "Turns out the RDC has been watching the *Rapscallion's Heart* for some time."

"I can explain," Vane said, no longer struggling in Velko's grip.

"Yeah?" Velko said, shoving him towards the open crate. "Maybe you can start with those."

She barged him into the container so he was forced to look down at the racks of blasters that had been hidden under the souvenirs.

"That's simple," hissed Sskeer, fixing Vane with a glare. "Your friend has been running weapons... for the Nihil."

TO BE CONTINUED...

Past Mistakes

PART TWO

Starlight Beacon had changed so much in such a short span of time. When she had first arrived, Administrator Velko Jahen had been taken aback by the atmosphere, everyone so confident and calm in the midst of such bustle. And then there was the excitement. You could feel it in the air. The Beacon was a fresh start, both for the galactic frontier and for a jaded veteran looking for a new purpose in life. Now? Now was different. All that had been before Valo. All that had been before the Jedi had been tasked with taking down the Nihil. It was before the wings of the security tower were packed with Nihil captured as part of Operation: Counterstrike.**

Now she was standing in front of a cell, looking at a man she had fought alongside back on Soika. A man she had, if not loved, cared for deeply. A man who was her prisoner. She had brought him in herself. She had clapped the binders on his wrists after discovering that he was using Starlight to run weapons for the Nihil, and she had one burning question.

"Why?"

Vane Sarpo sat with his back to her behind the energy field, his assistant Clune curled into a little orange ball, the instinctive reaction of all Peasles in moments of great peril. The small insectoid hadn't unfurled once since the smuggled blasters had been found.

"I need to know, Vane. Why do it? What did they offer you?"

The tattooed Vuman didn't answer, but the Nihil in the other cells certainly had a lot to say for themselves, jeering and shouting, one particularly scraggy Wookiee telling Velko in no uncertain terms what she would do to her if the energy fields failed. Velko wasn't worried. The guard at the door to the block had his stunstick and she had her blaster. She had made sure she was armed. The visit wasn't exactly authorized, and she was certain Security Chief Ghal Tarpfen would have a lot to say about it, but Velko wasn't taking any chances.

Still Vane remained silent. Nothing about this made sense to Velko. The thought that he might have willingly joined the Nihil was too terrible to comprehend. Vane had skirted close to various lines over the years, especially when they served together on Soika, she as a member of the Liberation Force and he as a mercenary, but he sure as hell wasn't an anarchist.

"Are they paying you, is that what it is?" No response. "Do you owe them money?" Still nothing. "For void's sake, Vane, talk to me."

Someone finally spoke, but it wasn't the prisoner.

"Administrator Jahen."

Velko swore under her breath as she heard the heavy footsteps behind her. She turned to see the imposing form of Jedi Master Sskeer striding towards her, his one good hand resting on his lightsaber hilt. "This," the Trandoshan hissed, "is most... irregular."

He was rattled, she could see that immediately. Something else that had changed since coming to Starlight. Before she'd believed that Jedi were incapable of emotion, a proposition that was just plain wrong. The Jedi she'd met felt as deeply as everyone else. They were just better at controlling it. At least, the majority were. Sskeer seemed to struggle more than most, and as for Marshal Avar Kriss...

"Master Jedi," she began, cutting off her thoughts. "I just thought—"

"You just thought you would use your personal history as leverage against the prisoner."

Velko's silver cheeks burned. "No, it wasn't like that."

"Of course it was," a voice said behind her, Vane speaking up at last. He still had his back to them, but there was an edge to his voice that she'd never heard before. "I would do the same, but you're wasting your time, Vel."

She couldn't believe that. "We can help you Vane, if you help us."

"If I help you, how?" He was on his feet now. "By spilling the secrets of the Nihil? And what would you do then, Administrator? Protect me, like the Jays protected Valo? You're a joke, you and your Jedi friends." His eyes darted between the two of them. "Look at you, in all your finery. Golden robes and starched collars. You will burn. You know that, don't you? All this will come crashing down around your heads. You can't help me, because you're the problem!"

All around, the imprisoned Nihil whooped in support of Vane's rant, the Wookiee shaking long matted arms above her head. What had Velko been thinking? This was useless. Vane... Vane wasn't the man she thought he was. The man he'd been. And if he wanted to rot in a Republic jail, so be it. She had work to do. Important work. Work helping bring down more men like him.

She turned on her heel, marching towards the guard at the door, pausing only when she realized that Sskeer wasn't with her. He was standing motionless outside Vane's cell.

"Master Sskeer?" she asked, but still, he didn't move. "Master Sskeer, are you coming?"

"Something isn't right," he said, ignoring the question, slitted orange eyes never leaving Vane's face. "I sense anger."

"Ha!" Vane barked, throwing up his arms in pantomime. "They weren't lying about you Jedi, were they? The lizard can tell I'm angry. And there was me thinking he was nothing more than a stupid dewback."

"We should go," Velko said to the Trandoshan.

"Finally she gets it," Vane snorted. "Give the girl a medal for her collection. Go on. Get out. You make me sick, the lot of you. Sick to my stomach."

"I sense more than anger," Sskeer continued, his words strangely pained. "I sense shame. I sense... fear."

There was something about the way the Jedi spoke that sent a chill through Velko, that the emotions he described were all too familiar. But Jedi didn't fear, did they? Sskeer was right though. Vane was afraid, she could see it in his eyes, but of what? Being locked up for his crimes? Of the repercussions if he betrayed the Nihil. No. It was something else. *Someone* else.

Vane's eyes flicked down to Clune and widened. The Peasle was rocking in her shell, preparing to unfurl.

Sskeer's lightsaber ignited.

"Drop the energy field," he ordered the guard at the door.

Vane raised his arms, palms out to the azure blade. "No. Don't do that. Get out. Please, get out."

"I won't ask again," Sskeer rumbled.

Velko looked back to the panicked guard, who was obviously wondering whether he should obey the Jedi or not. That's when a light flashed from inside Vane's cell.

It all happened so fast. Velko turned, her eyes opening wide as she realized that the glow was emanating from Vane Sarpo himself, the tattoos on his face flaring like jagged lightning.

"The field," Sskeer shouted, his nostrils flaring as the block filled with nauseating aromas of burning flesh and charred ozone. "Now!"

"No," Velko yelled, screwing up her eyes against the glare. "Lockdown the block. Lockdown the entire tower," she ordered.

The guard dived for the controls as light brighter than a sun burst from Vane's cell. Burst from Vane himself.

Velko cried out, throwing a hand across her eyes, but the damage was already done. She could only pray that the effects were only temporary, that she hadn't been blinded when her former lover had... what? Exploded? Her ears rang, but she could still make out the crackle of the security guard's stunstick and the shriek of Sskeer's lightsaber. Only one thing was noticeable by its absence – the hum of the energy fields that kept the prisoners at bay.

Blinking furiously, she pulled her blaster, squeezing off a few shots at the blurry shapes that raced towards her, the Nihil dropping to the floor. She aimed and fired without seeing, relying on her training, hearing the grunts and thuds of one fallen foe before turning on the next. It was only a matter of time before her luck ran out, a Nihil avoiding her shot, the blaster knocked from her hand. She heard it skid away and lashed out blindly, her fist finding only air. The Nihil had no problem connecting with Velko's jaw, sending a supernova of impossible colors flaring across her already muddled vision. She went down and they were on her, no matter how hard she thrashed and kicked. She was dragged up onto her knees, her arms twisted behind her, a rasped voice in her ear telling her to quit struggling. Like she had any choice. But even as her vision slowly cleared, her eyes streaming, a grin spread over her split lips. Sskeer would get them out of this. Sskeer was a Jedi. Sskeer had a lightsaber.

A lightsaber she could no longer hear.

Sskeer thudded to the deck to her right, pinned to the floor by the shaggy Wookiee who was obviously stronger than she looked. But they weren't done yet. Sskeer would use the Force. He would fling the Nihil from his back as easily as shrugging off his cloak.

Any minute now.

Any minute...

"Well, this is a quite a situation."

Tiny legs skittered on the floor as a Peasle scuttled around in front of them, a Peasle holding the guard's stunstick.

"Clune?" Velko gasped in shock.

"Hello there," the tiny insectoid said. "We didn't get a chance to chat before, did we?"

"Before you curled up into a ball," she reminded her.

"Like a coward," Sskeer added.

Clune shook her segmented head. "Such prejudice, from a Jedi of all people." The Peasle skittered over to Sskeer, prodding him with the stunstick which crackled with energy. The Trandoshan roared in pain, but Clune only tutted. "I don't mind saying, I am a little disappointed. It seems most undignified."

"The guard?" Velko asked, craning to look around. "Where is he?"

"Oh, he's dead," Clune informed her. "Quite, quite dead, but not before he managed to lock the doors, those our ion burst didn't knock out, that is."

Still fighting against the Nihil who was holding her tight, Velko twisted to peer into Vane's cell. The Vuman was sprawled face down, tendrils of smoke curling from his hidden face.

"Vane's tattoos," she croaked.

"Now those were clever," Clune said, her voice full of shrill pride. "Laced with ion filaments, don't you know? Rigged to detonate at a moment's notice, thanks to this." She jangled the control bangle that was slung loosely around one of her many wrists.

"How?" Velko asked.

A smile broke across the Peasle's segmented face. "It's remarkably hard to unfurl a Peasle once they've gone into a ball."

"What about the security scans?" Sskeer said.

"Next to useless," Clune confirmed. "Peasle chitin is equally effective at blocking sensor sweeps and, well, who suspects a... how did you put it, Jedi? 'A coward?'"

"Fascinating," Velko said through gritted teeth, "but not what I meant. How did you persuade Vane to do it? To tattoo his skin. To attack Starlight?"

Clune laughed, a thin chirruping sound. "He didn't really have any choice. I told you the tattoos were clever. Not only did they hide an ion charge; they could cause excruciating pain if he didn't do what I say. I must admit, I was impressed, the way he tried to get you to leave. All that shouting and carrying on. He must have really cared for you, not wanting you to be caught up in all..." the Peasle waved the stunstick in a circle that took in the entire cell block, "...in all this. Perhaps I underestimated him. Not that it matters. The filaments were a one-time deal. I'd hoped to detonate them in the middle of the night."

"But I forced your hand," Sskeer rumbled.

"Indeed you did, which brings us back to our problem. The whole idea was to escape."

"And now you're trapped," Velko said, allowing herself a bitter grin.

"We all are, my dear. Including you, all because you ordered the lockdown. Now we have no comms and no way out of here."

"But we do have this." A broad-headed Amanin Nihil walked in front of Sskeer and Velko, holding out a very familiar weapon with his gangly arm.

"Ah yes," Clune said, taking the hilt. "The Jedi's lightsaber."

"Don't you dare..." Sskeer growled, attempting, and failing, to push himself up from beneath the Wookiee.

"Don't you dare... what?" Clune asked. "Do this?"

Velko winced as the Peasle struck Sskeer across the face with his own knuckle guard.

"Or this?"

The blue blade slid majestically from the hilt, its light reflected in Clune's eyes. All the time, Sskeer fought to stand, but was kept pinned to the floor.

"This is what's going to happen," Clune said, slowly swinging the blade around so it was dangerously close to Velko's face. "We're going to bargain for your life. Either they let us all go, or you'll start losing limbs." She sniggered, before glancing back to Sskeer. "*More* limbs in some cases."

"No," Velko said quietly.

"What's that?"

She looked Clune straight in her black eyes. "It doesn't matter what you do to me, I won't help you, and neither will the Jedi. You'll be captured and thrown back into your cell with no means to escape."

"Is that so?" the Peasle asked, bringing the glowing blade ever closer. There was no heat, but that wouldn't stop it burning as soon as the containment field touched her skin. Velko screwed up her eyes, bracing herself for the pain... pain that never came.

A blaster bolt flared out of nowhere, spinning Clune around, the lit saber flying from her hand. The second shot struck her square in the back and she went down, the dead guard's stunstick clattering to the floor.

Velko didn't look to see who had fired. She didn't have time. She brought her head back sharply, connecting with the jaw of the Nihil who was holding her. They staggered back, losing their grip and she pounced, snatching up the stunstick and bringing it around to jab it hard into the Wookiee's side. The shaggy Nihil cried out as volts flowed freely through her body, Sskeer finally able to push himself free. The saber was in his hand within seconds, Velko and the Jedi standing shoulder to shoulder, weapons bared and ready to punish any Nihil who dared attack.

But none of them even moved. Maybe it was the double-threat of saber and stunstick, or the fact that the Nihil had lost the advantage. More likely it had something to do with the blaster held in Vane Sarpo's hand, ready to cut them down at a moment's notice. Velko had no idea if Vane had fallen on her weapon by accident, or purposely covered it with his body as he regained his strength, but it didn't matter, not now that he was smiling grimly at her, his faced badly burned.

"Clune was right," he wheezed, his eyes sparkling through the pain. "No one ever thinks to check the coward."

***

The guards arrived minutes later, along with Sskeer's former Padawan, Keeve Trennis, who never seemed far from her master's side. Vane was transferred to a secure wing in the medicenter, his burns dressed, and any trace of the Nihil tattoos removed from his face. Sskeer himself insisted on guarding the room, but Velko had a sneaking suspicion that he was more concerned in protecting Vane from Nihil reprisals than the Vuman making a run for it.

"I'm sorry," Vane said to her from his bed.

"That you got caught?" she said, trying not to smile. "Although I guess that was the general idea."

He shrugged. "Hard to spring a security block of Nihil if you're still standing in the hangar bay."

"You could have trusted me, you know? You could have told me what was happening, back in the bar."

"Could I?" He touched his cheek, flinching slightly.

"It wasn't toothache," she said, remembering him wincing at the time. "It was a warning."

He nodded. "Clune reminding me to get back to business. Which you should do too." He broke into that infuriating smile. "Especially if you're going to get me a pardon."

"Already sorted, but it wasn't me." She nodded to Sskeer standing with his broad back to them at the door.

"The old dewback has a heart?"

"The old dewback has excellent hearing too," the Trandoshan rumbled without moving.

"Then, thank you," Vane told him, before looking back at Velko. "To both of you."

"I'll check back with you later," Velko said, heading for the door. "Don't go anywhere, you hear?"

"I'll see what I can do." Vane was starting to sound more like himself, even though doubt crept into his voice as he called out: "Vel?"

She stopped, looking at him propped up in bed.

"Are you really happy here? With all this going on? With the Nihil and the Jedi and the..."

She'd shrugged off the question last time he'd asked, sitting in Unity's. This time she didn't even hesitate, even after everything that had happened in the last few hours. Because of what happened. So what if life on the Beacon had become more difficult? Starlight was here to offer hope, to protect, to stop things like Valo happening again.

And so was she.

"Yes," she said, meaning it with all her heart. "I wouldn't be anywhere else."

THE END

Shadows Remain

PART ONE

By Justina Ireland

Ghal Tarpfen, head of security on Starlight Beacon, was dreaming. She knew it wasn't real, because instead of the gleaming metal corridors of the station her surroundings were an iridescent pink shell. She was somehow back on Mon Cala, dressed in the garb of the royal guard: flowing kelp gauntlets, fitted scrye-fish skin tunic and trousers, feet bare to better swim through difficult currents.

In the dream Ghal stood at attention in an anteroom she didn't remember, even though her subconscious did.

"Ghal Tarpfen, daughter of Rhal and Gera, Captain Third Class of the Royal Guard. Please approach."

Dream Ghal was filled with a sort of quivering excitement about being summoned to the dais by the regal figure of Shenrick, who sat there with a crown that should not have belonged to him. But real Ghal could feel the sorrow that this moment was about to deliver, and she grieved once more.

Ah, thought Ghal, watching her dream self approach the dais in the center of the room, *this one again.*

Ghal did not know how others dreamed. She'd watched her co-worker, Velko Jahen, doze off once or twice during long shifts in the command hub, and the silver-skinned, silver-haired Soikan seemed to be wholly consumed by her sleeping visions, but for Ghal her dreams always left her with a strange sense of detachment. It was odd that this dream should feel so immediate.

But perhaps that was because it was less a dream and more a memory. And a painful one at that. She'd had this same dream more than a dozen times since arriving on Starlight Beacon more than a year ago, and their increasing frequency was beginning to unnerve Ghal.

What warning was her subconscious trying to impart to her that she had not yet heeded?

"Ghal, we are truly in awe of the service you have provided the crown these past few turns," the figure on the dais said. The Mon Calamari there had no face, even though real Ghal knew the peaks and valleys of his visage. "And it is with a heavy heart that we grant your request to be removed from your service to the crown."

This was the part where dream Ghal drew back in shock, desperately trying to keep the hurt from her face. She hadn't seen the betrayal coming, she never did.

But what else had she expected from falling in love with a male too far above her station?

"Ghal! Did you hear me?"

Ghal startled awake, the watery filter of the dream evaporating as she came back to herself.

"I was asleep."

"That's the third time this shift. Maybe you should call it a day. Or a night," Velko said with a forced laugh. "What time is it, even?"

"Not until I finish this report," Ghal said, turning back to her terminal.

Not far away Velko Jahen watched Ghal with a slight frown. Their relationship had been strained ever since the incident with Velko's former lover, Vane Sarpo. Ghal would almost swear that was what was causing her nightmares, because that's what they were, reliving that moment when the love of her life had cast her aside. But she'd been having the nighttime visions long before the issue with the Nihil in the security block.

"Ghal—" Velko began again, but Ghal held up a hand.

"You have my attention, Administrator Jahen," Ghal said. Formality was a safe fallback. "I will depart for my rest, shortly. Is there anything else?"

Velko shifted uncomfortably. The Soikan wore her emotions too obviously, an open data file for anyone to read. "Look, Ghal, about the incident in the security block—"

"We're past that," Ghal said. She didn't want Velko's apologies, especially not when the pain of the dream was so fresh. "What seems to be amiss?" She tried to soften her tone, so that Velko would not start up once more with her blasted apologies.

"We have a new official on board and the Jedi are requesting a secured berth. Vice President Hackrack Bep, from Dalna."

"All planetary officials require secured berths while on official business, that's nothing new. We'll put him in the same wing as Senator Starros," Ghal said.

"Yes, that's what I figured. But I keep getting an error from the security suite in corridor sixteen. Have you ever seen anything like this?"

Ghal stood from her chair, taking a moment to stretch before going to stand behind Velko where the administrator sat at her workstation and watched the code flow past. After a moment Ghal reached over Velko's shoulder and typed in a couple lines of commands. There was a beep and a whirring sound, and then the status came back as normal, feeds from the cameras populating the screen once more.

"Looks like one of the security droids shut down the hall cams. Strange. They aren't supposed to do such a thing." Ghal burbled a bit, the Mon Calamari equivalent of a yawn. "I'll check on it when I get back from the refresher."

"Go ahead and catch some rest as well," Velko said, swallowing a yawn of her own. "That report will wait, and we're all tired. Things will just have to take a little longer. I think the Republic will understand. I'll grab a break when you get back."

Ghal nodded and walked off without another word. The last few weeks had been incredibly busy. The Jedi had rounded up hundreds of Nihil and all Starlight Beacon officials had been working double shifts to accommodate the influx of prisoners. The Jedi were very careful not to kill the Nihil if they could help it, which meant that Velko, Ghal, and every other Republic administrator on Starlight Beacon had seen their workload increase. Processing criminals required a number of forms, and since none of the Nihil ever gave their true name they were also spending a ridiculous amount of time capturing an image of each pirate to run through the databank of known felons. It was tiresome work, and they still had the day-to-day running of Starlight to attend to.

It made rest a prize to be treasured, so Ghal was not going to argue when Velko offered to let her take the first sleep shift.

Instead, she hurried out of the command hub before Velko changed her mind.

***

After a visit to the refresher and a restorative dip in the springs set aside for such things, Ghal returned to her room and prepared for her rest cycle. She had barely submerged herself in her sleeping tank, her head bobbing above the water, before she was in the nightmare once more. This time Shenrick peered down at her, his face no longer distorted. Now, she could see his bulbous eyes and mottled skin, his markings the same ones she had fallen in love with when he was just a useless third son with no future.

"Thank you for your service," he said, his voice strange, and her heart broke anew, both in the dream and in real life.

Ghal startled awake, shaking off the remnants of the dream as she rolled over in the tank, her neck pillow keeping her head above the water line. The timer she'd set still hadn't expired, but there would be no more sleeping. Not after the nightmare. This was twice in a very short span. There was a warning here, and Ghal knew that she wouldn't be able to sleep any more with the vision of Shenrick's cold expression lingering in her mind. Velko would just get a longer rest shift.

Ghal rose from the tank, dressed, and headed back to the command hub, only stopping long enough to see if her boss, Rodor Keen, was in his office. Rodor oversaw all of the operations on Starlight Beacon, and something about the way the cameras had powered down in corridor sixteen niggled at her. Perhaps it was the aftermath of the nightmare, the memory of the worst day of her life, but there was something amiss. If anyone would know what could cause such an error, Rodor would.

Unfortunately, his droid informed her that he was also resting and would be back momentarily, so Ghal left a message and made her way back to her post.

Velko looked up as Ghal walked in, her expression relieved. "Oh good. I didn't want to wake you, but a message came in from the Republic security liaison with an urgent code. I put it in your queue."

"Why didn't you just read it and respond?" Ghal asked, her normally short temper even shorter. She already had a dozen reports to file, and interviews to conduct. She didn't need more work.

Velko gave Ghal a wan smile. "It was keyed to your access code."

Ghal Tarpfen looked at the holo before her and frowned. Velko said something but Ghal didn't hear her, all of her attention focused on the missive before her. She didn't even notice the Soikan leave.

The holomessage in Ghal's queue was encrypted and bore a messaging signature that was reserved for members of the Senate, not the Republic security office as Velko had thought. Still, it was strange. There was nothing about the message that was any different than the usual traffic they got, warnings of Nihil activity or new Hutt smuggling routes to patrol. So why had the message been flagged for Ghal?

The holo queue blinked at her, the unplayed message still waiting, and with a sigh Ghal played the holo. It flickered as it played, as though the sending signal hadn't been very strong, and the person in the message wore a mask like the Nihil. A vocalizer disguised the voice of the speaker, whose species could not easily be distinguished, but they looked to Ghal to be human.

"During the nocturnal rest cycle you will disable the cameras to the following corridors: sixteen, twenty-three, eighty-four. We know who you once were, and we trust that you would like to keep your secrets. For the Storm!"

Ghal played the message a few more times, trying to memorize as much about it as she could. But there was nothing in the holo, or on the sending information, to tell Ghal just who was responsible for the message. It did not escape Ghal's attention that corridor sixteen was the same one where the droids had already deactivated the cameras once.

She did not believe in coincidences.

Ghal ran a security check on the messaging encryption, but the information came back as legitimate. Smart. Whoever had sent it wanted her to know that the Nihil had friends in very high places, the kind of places that could utterly destroy Ghal if she didn't go along with what they wanted.

She suddenly felt ill.

All of the weeks spent dreaming about Shenrick. Was this what her mind wanted to warn her about? When Ghal was a child she used to like to sit in the currents outside of her house and see the things the ocean brought to her door, which was mostly just bits of flotsam from the well-to-do families who lived up current. One day there had been a dead jara fish that had drifted by in bits and pieces, a gruesome discovery that she'd been powerless to look away from. First a fin, then the tail, and finally a whole head, the eyes wide staring and confused, like the fish wondered how its demise had come to pass. Ghal felt that way now, like she'd been dismembered and set adrift in the current. It was not a good feeling.

She was half tempted to delete the holo, but had a feeling that somehow they would know. And now the random holos she'd received over the past few months began to make sense. They had seemed like mistakes: snippets of Mon Calamari gossip sites detailing the king's latest social events, documentary excerpts of features on the Mon Calamari guard, and—most alarming of all—a holodrama from years ago featuring a Mon Calamari guard and a princess who fell in love and ran off together.

Ghal knew that vid by heart. Hadn't she and Shen watched the holo and talked about how it was *their* story?

But that was before Shenrick had ascended to the throne, the spare become the heir after a terrible tragedy. And that was before Ghal had pledged her troth to the Republic, a position in a far away outpost better than staying and watching Shenrick marry another after being cast aside.

Somehow, the Nihil had learned her secret, had pieced it together. Ghal had nothing to fear from the discovery, her time with the Royal Guard was nothing more than a delightful footnote to the Republic. But the purists on Mon Cala would be aghast if they knew their king hadn't been pure before ascending to the throne. Shenrick would be ruined, of course, and while part of Ghal yearned for his casual cruelty toward her to be turned back on him tenfold, it would destroy her family. After all, the Mon Calamari could not wholly blame their king for such a misstep. Her family was low enough in standing that they would bear the brunt of raising an honorless daughter, and Ghal would not disgrace her line.

"Ghal!" Velko said, her voice exasperated as though she had been trying to get Ghal's attention for more than a moment.

"Apologies," Ghal burbled. "Too much kelp gathering, I'm afraid."

"I brought you this," the Soikan said, setting down a cup of the kelp tea Ghal liked. "I'm going to take my rest period. But will you check in with Senator Starros in the next hour or so? She's been requesting assistance non-stop, and sending in dozens of complaints."

Ghal sighed. "Senators. I'll stop by her quarters and she what it is she wants."

Velko stood to go, and paused, her gaze searching Ghal. "Is everything okay?"

"Fine," Ghal said. She picked up the cup Velko had set down and took a sip. "I think I just need to visit the restorative springs. Thank you for the kelp tea."

Velko nodded and departed, leaving Ghal with nothing but her runaway thoughts. There was a senator on Starlight and she'd just been asked to disable the cameras in the area.

There was nothing okay about that.

Ghal tasked one of the security droids with scanning the feeds and hurried to Senator Starros' guest suite. Would the Nihil try to kill a senator? Perhaps. But not on her watch.

The ride in the lift seemed to take forever, and by the time Ghal reached corridor sixteen she could tell there was something wrong. It was the middle of the sleep cycle, but one of the doors was curiously open, as though someone had jammed the mechanism.

Ghal drew her blaster and crept toward the open door. It wasn't one that opened out into the suite of rooms occupied by the senator, but by someone else entirely. Ghal peered around the corner. Lying on the ground was a Theelin man Ghal did not recognize.

"Oh, Ghal," someone burbled in poorly spoken Mon Calamari, a language Ghal had not heard since she'd left home. Ghal whirled around to see a stately human woman with dark skin smiling at her. She was vaguely familiar, but Ghal could not quite place her. "You should've just done as you were told."

Ghal drew her blaster, but before she could do anything a heavy hand hit her from behind, and it was only as she was falling that she realized she knew the woman after all.

Senator Ghirra Starros was apparently quite a bit more than she seemed.

TO BE CONCLUDED...

Shadows Remain

PART TWO

By Justina Ireland

Velko Jahen sat in the security hub of Starlight Beacon staring at her terminal and checking the scans once again. It had been three days since anyone had seen Ghal Tarpfen, Starlight Beacon's head of security, and Velko was beginning to fear the worst.**

Ghal might actually be a traitor.

All the evidence pointed to that logical conclusion, but Velko's gut told her quite the opposite. Ghal was prickly and curt, but she respected the Republic and did things by the book. Could someone so worried about protocol really participate in an assassination attempt?

A few days ago, someone had attacked a visiting dignitary, Vice President Hackrack Bep, an official from the planet of Dalna. He had arrived on Starlight in the company of Jedi Padawan Imri Cantaros, seeking aid because of suspected Nihil activity. That wasn't out of the ordinary. As the Jedi and the Republic had pushed the space pirates to the brink of desperation with continued operations against their marauding, more and more planets had sought assistance, but it was odd that the official had been attacked in his rooms so shortly after his arrival. He had no memory of the assault, and the only video clips that showed any evidence had been erased by Ghal, her security number clearly recorded in the logs.

Velko had flagged the activity for further investigation, but the droid assigned to the task had found no anomalies in the data. With the emergency on Dalna, which had forced Starlight Beacon to be towed through hyperspace to render aid, Velko had not yet been able to fully debrief Rodor Keen on the exact nature of Ghal's disappearance. And now that it was time, she was hesitant.

There was less than an hour until Velko was scheduled to meet with the highest-ranking Republic official on Starlight. Velko had planned on telling the man that the most logical conclusion was that Ghal had been working with the Nihil, but now she wasn't so sure.

If Ghal was working with the Nihil, what would she have to gain from it? There were no deposits of credits into any of her financial accounts, and a search of Ghal's quarters had turned up nothing suspicious.

Velko looked at the information one last time—the deletion of the assault, the strange nature of the messages in Ghal's message queue—and willed the information to turn into something less incriminating, anything but a clear picture that Ghal Tarpfen was a traitor.There had to be a better explanation.

***

Ghal Tarpfen woke with a start. She tensed as she realized she was bound to a chair by her wrists, in the galley of a ship she didn't recognize. The star-strewn darkness beyond a nearby viewport told her all she needed to know. She was in a very bad spot.

Ghal's skin felt dry, tight and itchy, a common occurrence when she'd taken too long to visit a mister, so she estimated she must have been out for at least a day, if not longer. Her head was heavy and achy, a feeling she'd never experienced before, and she wondered if she'd been subjected to some sort of knockout gas. The last thing she remembered was confronting Senator Ghirra Starros in the doorway to some other official's room, which meant the senator must have had an accomplice.

Ghal took in her surroundings, ignoring the rising panic making her heart pound.

Judging by the sparkling surfaces of the galley, the ship looked like it was a newer model, especially considering the smart food prep unit mounted to a nearby counter. Everything was shiny and pristine. Testing her bonds, Ghal decided struggling was futile. She needed to conserve her strength. Someone was flying the ship, and at some point they would come to check on her. When they did, Ghal would be ready. The fact that she was still alive was a good sign. It meant that they thought they had use for her. It meant there was still a fighting chance.

Sure enough, a while later the door slid open, admitting a rough-looking Aqualish woman, the dark orbs of her single pair of eyes and a set of mandibles dominating her face.

"You wake. Good," she said between grunts and growls. "We land soon."

"I... where are we?" Ghal asked.

"No Space. Senator has use for you. So, you'll be kept alive as long as needed."

Ghal said nothing. They had to be Nihil—who else would make a trip to No Space?—and she wouldn't help them with anything. Despite the newness of the ship, the Aqualish had the rough look of those space pirates. Her clothing was designed purely for survival, and the filter apparatus that dangled from her neck had the distinct look of a gas mask.

But more interesting was the silver key fob dangling from her trousers. Most likely the key to her restraints. The Republic used a similar system, and Ghal was well trained in how the key fob functioned. It was the first ray of hope she'd had since she'd awakened.

"Can I get some water," Ghal said, her voice extra croaky. "I... need water."

"You wait until we land."

"I'm sorry. I can't..." Ghal said, trailing off. She tried to make her voice sound weak. "Please. I don't know how long I've been out, but my skin is so dry."

That was true, though while her skin felt uncomfortable Ghal was not in any kind of danger from lack of moisture. Not that the Aqualish knew that.

The woman sneered at Ghal but went to a nearby cabinet and pulled out a bottle with a spritzer attachment. She approached Ghal, who lashed out with a kick as soon as the Aqualish was close enough. Ghal's wrists had been bound, but her feet had not. The kick landed well, catching the woman in her mandibles and knocking her unconcious. Ghal used the tip of her toes to tap the fob until her restraints unlocked, freeing her.

One problem solved, innumerable more to handle.

Ghal searched the woman quickly for weapons; finding none, she picked her up and put her in the chair she had just vacated, locking her into the restraints.

It turned out that Ghal was actually parched. She went to the food unit and ordered enough water that she could drink a bit and pour the rest over her head, not trusting whatever the Aqualish woman had been about to spray her with.

And then Ghal set out to see just what kind of Nihil the ship contained.

***

Velko paced outside of Rodor Keen's office as she waited for him to finish up his daily meeting with the marshal of Starlight, Jedi Avar Kriss. When Kriss finally exited, the pale-skinned human woman sparing the Soikan administrator a nod of acknowledgement, Velko hurried into the controller's office. She was surprised to find

Jedi Master Estala Maru still speaking with Rodor.

"Oh. Should I come back?" Velko asked, and Rodor waved her over.

"No. Master Maru is here for the same reason you are."

"Ghal Tarpfen," The Jedi Master said, the Kessurian male's face twisted with concern. "She's not on Starlight Beacon."

"No." Velko began. "It seems like she's fled."

"Someone was extorting her," Maru said. "Did you have any clue?"

Velko shook her head. "No. I knew something was wrong, but even before the hyperspace tow and the Dalnan refugee crisis we were spread thin. Processing the Nihil, we've been picking up and trying to make sure all of our regular duties were accounted for." Velko sighed. "I should've noticed something was amiss." She and Ghal weren't friends, and Velko wasn't silly enough to think that the Mon Calamari woman would have confided in her. But perhaps if she hadn't been so wrapped up in her duties she could've noted the change in Ghal's behavior before things got bad.

Velko didn't believe she couldn't have helped.

The Jedi nodded; his expression pensive. "It seems as though it was mostly benign, but she was getting a number of messages from the same exchange. I've tried locating where they originated, but I'm still waiting on the droid to return with the answer."

"If Ghal was being extorted then she might have gone after the people responsible," Rodor said. "Did you find any footage of her leaving Starlight?"

Velko shook her head, looking to the Jedi. But he was similarly vexed. "No. There's no sign of her departure."

"Ghal Tarpfen is a competent woman," Rodor finally said after a long silence. "Let's just hope that wherever she's gotten to we can help her when she needs it."

***

Ghal stalked through the ship, checking compartments and listening for the telltale sound of boots approaching. But the ship seemed to be empty, so Ghal doubled back to the cockpit to see just who was flying the thing.

A Chagrian woman sat at the yoke. Ghal tried to sneak up on her, but the woman somehow sensed her and spun around. Ghal lashed out with a fist before the woman could finish standing, but she was able to easily block the punch, landing one of her own to Ghal's unprotected midsection.

"Ghal. You're supposed to be in the galley," the woman said as Ghal gasped for breath. The Mon Calamari woman leapt backward to avoid a kick, and Ghal was able to take the opportunity to land a low kick of her own.

The Chagrian woman fell to the ground, and Ghal was on her immediately, kneeling on her chest so that she couldn't move. The woman struggled, and Ghal pulled one of the woman's lethorns and twisted it until she yelped.

"I know you," Ghal said, once the woman had stilled. "Jeni Wataro. You work for Senator Izzet Noor."

The woman laughed. "I work for myself. And when it suits me, for the Eye."

An alarm began to sound in the cockpit, and Jeni began to cackle. "That's an alert that we're about to encounter another ship. And where we are, I guarantee it won't be anyone from the Republic."

Ghal pushed her forearm against Jeni's throat, making the woman gasp for breath. It

wasn't an elegant way to subdue an opponent, but Ghal was pressed for time. Jeni struggled and tried to throw Ghal off of her, but eventually her struggles fell away to nothing.

Ghal checked the woman to make sure she was still breathing, and once she was satisfied she hadn't killed Jeni she dragged her body clear of the cockpit door, closing and latching the thing so she wouldn't be disturbed.

Ghal was not a very good pilot, and she hadn't flown in what felt like years. The controls meant next to nothing to her, and she took a moment to stare at the various knobs and dials, which were labeled in something other than Galactic Basic.

Ghal's remaining hope evaporated, and she swore long and loud. How in the deepest sea was she supposed to turn this thing back toward Starlight?

Ghal took the yoke, and tried to turn the ship to another course, but she very quickly realized that the settings were locked somehow. Fumbling with a number of switches and buttons did nothing, and Ghal sat back in the seat, a keen sense of defeat coming over her. The last time she had felt this helpless was when her former lover, now a King of Mon Cala, had put her aside.

The beeping in the cockpit grew more insistent, and Ghal saw three approaching ships. How long would it be before they began to fire upon her vessel? The comm unit blinked at her as someone tried to open a channel with the ship, but Ghal ignored it. There was no way she could take on three ships worth of Nihil. She'd lost. The Nihil had won.

Ghal closed her eyes, took a deep breath and opened them once more. There had to be something she could do, something to at least warn the Republic that there were dangers lurking in the kelp. First Senator Ghirra Starros, and now Jeni Wataro. How many others in the Senate were working with the Nihil for their own purposes?

Ghal didn't know, but she opened a comms channel, selecting a wide swath of frequencies to ping to, most of them Starlight Beacon frequencies, but a few Mon Cal that she remembered from her Royal Guard days. This far out in No Space she would be lucky if even one person heard her message.

Ghal took a deep breath, and opened the channels, sending a simple voice message since it was far more likely to get where someone could hear it. "My name is Ghal Tarpfen, Head of Security for Starlight Beacon. I have been kidnapped by the Nihil, and by the time you hear this message I will most likely be dead. But you must know that the Senate is compromised. At least two members there have been working with the Nihil: Senator Ghirra Starros of Hosnian Prime and Jeni Wataro, aide to Senator Izzet Noor of Serenno. Please be aware that there might be other spies in the Senate, and at all other levels of the Republic."

Ghal cleared her throat and repeated the message again, and again. When the first few blasts came from the approaching ships, she continued talking, repeating the message once more before putting it on a loop.

A pounding came from the door to the cockpit, followed by yelling in a language that Ghal didn't understand. There was some murmuring, as another shot rattled the ship down to its rivets.

"Unlock the escape shuttles, you horned squawkin!" came Jeni Wataro's voice through the door.

Ghal smiled, the first in a very long time. "Sorry, not sure I know how to do that."

"Then let me in to answer the challenge question! You're condemning us to death."

"I had family on Valo," Ghal yelled to be heard over the noise of the ship as another blast set off a fresh bout of alarms. The life support systems had been damaged in that last cannon hit, and it wouldn't be long until the ship failed utterly. "Do you think they begged for someone to save them as well?"

The pounding on the door ceased, and Ghal leaned back in the chair and began to sing the lullaby her mother had always sang for her when she was a small fry.

It was a better death than she could have hoped for.

***

Velko woke in the middle of her sleep shift, startled by something she couldn't name. She'd been dreaming, she was sure of that, but what about?

There was a pinging at her door, and when she went to open it she found Imri Cantaros, the Padawan who had helped to save the Dalnans when their volcanic system flooded the planet with lava.

"Administrator Velko," he said with a sheepish grin. "Master Maru tried calling you over the comms, but I guess you didn't hear. There's something he wants you to listen to."

"Give me a moment," Velko said, closing the door. She hurriedly donned her uniform and followed the Padawan to the command hub, where Maru presided over a number of monitors.

"Velko," Maru said, a kind expression on his face. "We have news."

He didn't say anything else, just went to a nearby comms unit and began to play a message.

"Ghal Tarpfen…kidnapped…Nihil…Senate is compromised… there might be other spies… the Republic."

The message began to repeat, and Velko frowned. There were few words, the majority of the transmission was static. "What is the rest of the message? What are we missing?"

"I'm not sure. This is all we have been able to recover. I'm reaching out to other security units to see if they received anything similar, but I wanted to let you know first."

Velko nodded, the sinking feeling in her middle a heavy weight. Ghal was gone. There were few places in the galaxy far enough away that she might have trouble sending a message, and wherever she was had to be outside of Republic control. She knew her time was at an end, and yet she made every effort to send them a warning as her last act.

"Can you send a copy of that to my personal message queue?" Velko asked, and Maru nodded.

"I'm sorry about your loss," he said, and Velko left the command hub without another word, lost in her own dark thoughts.

She wandered around Starlight Beacon. There was still time in her sleep shift to rest, but she was no longer tired. She walked onto one of the observation decks, looking out and the seemingly endless expanse of stars beyond the transparisteel barrier.

Ghal might be gone, but her words were still there for Velko to parse and examine. Nihil spies in both the Senate and the Republic? How had Ghal found that out? Was that why she'd gone missing from Starlight?

Velko didn't know.

She sat on a bench and stared out into the vastness of space, letting the emotions swirl through her. In the months that she'd been on Starlight, Ghal Tarpfen had taught Velko more than the Mon Calamari woman would ever know. Ghal had been fierce and unyielding in her dedication to the Republic, and she was a fine head of security. During the Soikan Civil War, Velko had learned how important it was to have allies. Not friends, but something more: a person who could always be depended on to be there in the fight, someone who would watch your back. Ghal had been that for her, and now she was gone.

There was an answer to who had done this, and why. It could be the Nihil, Ghal didn't have any other enemies that Velko knew of, but either way there was an answer that needed to be found. Velko would find out who had taken Ghal and why, and

when she did she would make sure that Ghal's death got the justice it deserved.

But until then, Velko swore to herself that she would guide Starlight through any hardship that came next. It was what was right. It was what was needed.

She owed Ghal that much.

THE END

01

The Authors of *Star Wars: The High Republic*

KNIGHTS AT THE ROUNDTABLE

Insider assembled the group of talented creators behind *Star Wars: The High Republic* for a roundtable interview to talk Jedi Knights and a galaxy of potential.

WORDS: AMY RATCLIFFE

P*roject Luminous.* A mysterious phrase that crept into *Star Wars* authors' panel conversations and social media posts during *Star Wars* Celebration Chicago in 2019. Fans learned that multiple publishers would be involved with the ambitious initiative—as would authors Claudia Gray, Justina Ireland, Daniel José Older, Cavan Scott, and Charles Soule. After months of teasers, Lucasfilm finally pulled back the curtains on February 24, 2020 and unveiled the title of this new saga: *Star Wars: The High Republic*.

The stories of *The High Republic*, which debuted in January 2021, take place in a new era, some two hundred years before the events of *Star Wars: The Phantom Menace* (1999). Publishing partners including Del Rey, Marvel Comics, IDW Publishing, Disney Lucasfilm Press, and more will release stories set in this timeline—a timeline created in partnership with five top-flight authors and Lucasfilm. *Insider* spoke with the writers and Lucasfilm Publishing Creative Director Michael Siglain about the first phase.

***Star Wars Insider*: You all worked together at Skywalker Ranch to brainstorm. We've heard the food there is terrific. So first thing's first, is there a particular meal you each recall loving?**
Daniel José Older: I remember discovering the breakfast that they have, because there are multiple breakfasts. But there's one that they did in the tech building where they made eggs. Every day was something different, and what joy. What absolute joy.
Cavan Scott: I was having about three breakfasts a day, I think. I'd have the one in the guest house when I woke up early, because my head was still in U.K. time. Then they'd put out another buffet breakfast in the guest house so I'd have one of those. Then I'd wander to the tech building and have that one. I put on a few pounds.
Charles Soule: We were up there twice, and at the end of each time we would order a huge Chinese meal on the last night, and we would all get plates of it. Then we would sit outside at the inn. We would all just sit and chat, and it was just really nice. It's a beautiful place anyway, but it felt like the work was done and we were just all together. The food was fine, but the company was great.
Claudia Gray: Speak for yourself. The eclairs that we had the first day were amazing. They had mango puree. The company was fine; the food was great.
Justina Ireland: The main house buffet—it's pretty awesome. I'm a big fan of dessert, so that was my favorite part.

01 (Opposite page) Cavan Scott, Charles Soule, Claudia Gray, Daniel José Older, and Justina Ireland.

The High Republic is a huge cross-publisher event. Mike, how did you pitch the idea and then bring it all together?

Michael Siglain: The concept of a cross-publisher event was something I first pitched to Kathleen Kennedy and to Kiri Hart in 2014. It just took years of, "Can we do it now? Is now good? How about now?"

I had spoken to the publishers individually about the idea of doing something that would be unique to publishing—where we could have a corner of the galaxy that we could call our own—and everyone loved that concept. So, when we got toward the end of the Skywalker saga, Kathy said, "Okay, let's start this. What can you do in publishing?" She threw down the gauntlet. The one caveat was that it had to be a Lucasfilm-driven initiative. That allowed us a ton of creative freedom because then we were really in the driver's seat. So we looked to a bunch of current creators that we considered our all-star *Star Wars* authors to come and craft this initiative."

Then the icing on the cake was saying, "Now let's go up to Skywalker Ranch and bring together Story Group and the editorial team and spend a couple days talking about what we love about *Star Wars*, and creating a new era to play in."

Cavan, we heard you put an idea on the table that helped form the foundation of _The High Republic_. Is that true?

Scott: Well, what happened was that we all either came with an idea that was pre-formed, or we created an idea during our first week at the ranch. Toward the end of the week we each pitched in a general idea, then we went away and added meat to those bones, incorporating the ideas in. My initial idea came from the question: What scares the Jedi? That started us off, but then we began to pool ideas from the other pitches as well. We were working on quite an evolved version of it, with everyone else obviously throwing their ideas in.

In the prequel era, the Jedi Order is bound to the rules and tied closely into the Republic's politics. Is there a political factor to any of your _High Republic_ stories?

Soule: How we're approaching *The High Republic* is that it feels new and fresh. It's an optimistic society; it's a Republic that wants to explore its potential through the chancellor of the time, Lina Soh. She is extremely influential, but the scope of her influence comes from her optimism and her hope and her sense that everyone in the Republic is part of the same thing. The slogan that she has promulgated as her rallying cry for the Republic is, "We are all the Republic." That's something people say throughout all of the planets of the galaxy. The dividing lines that we see in the prequel era are between Separatists and so on. Those things don't exist here yet, and the idea is that it's a time when people can come together

02 Variant cover art for Marvel Comic's *The High Republic* issue #1 by Ario Anindito.

to bring the galaxy forward. Lina Soh has an expansive program of what are called "Great Works" that are designed to bring the High Republic to a new level, and also expand its principles and policies to new worlds.

Justina, your *High Republic* story, *A Test of Courage*, features the youngest Jedi we know, Vernestra Rwoh. What world-building did you get to explore with her?

Ireland: The inciting incident of the story is about this diplomatic envoy, these ambassadors going to the Inner Rim from the Outer Rim planets. These planets are not part of the Republic. When we get to *The Phantom Menace*, we see the Senate and there are hundreds and hundreds of planets represented. But at some point those planets had to decide to join the Republic, so, this is that period of expansion.

Part of that story is exploring what it looks like to be a young Jedi who gets sent on a diplomatic boondoggle, which is an official term, and things go wrong that have to be addressed. To have a kids' book that strips away those politics of the larger *Star Wars* era has always felt wrong. A lot of the conversation in the book is about what happens when certain people don't want to join the Republic. It's really about giving child characters a moment to have those very adult experiences in a more microcosm-type way, on a smaller scale. It's about reconciling the idea of, "I have these teachings behind me, but now I'm going up against people who don't have those same beliefs. How do we reconcile and realize that we all want the same thing? How do we look at our interactions with one another and make the best choice, not just for ourselves but for everyone?"

03 The authors with Mike Siglain and James Waugh, VP, franchise content & strategy (top row, third and fourth from the right) at *The High Republic* Launch.

Claudia, your book—*Into the Dark*—features another young Jedi going out on an adventure, but he isn't maybe as excited about it as others. Tell us more about him.

Gray: Reath is still a Padawan, unlike Vern, and he's looking forward to seeing her again as they're friends. But he really has been a little bit more sheltered than the average Padawan. His master is on the Jedi Council and has been much more centered on Coruscant than the average Jedi would be for that period of time. But now she's taken the job to be the head of Starlight Beacon, so he's going to the frontier, and he does not want to do that. He doesn't lack courage or ability, I want to be clear about that, but let's just say there are some of us that really, really like being around books. In chapter one he says, "Adventure is a euphemism for going places with lots of bugs." I think that's absolutely true.

He winds up with some adult Jedi being marooned on a very mysterious, very ancient space station that is full of surprises, dark and otherwise.

Flipping over to the comic book side of things, Daniel, who are the main crew we'll be spending time with in *The High Republic Adventures* from IDW Comics?

Older: One aspect I've been looking at very carefully is what it's like to be a young person in a time of gigantic change. Here, these kids who are on the front lines as young Jedi get to experience it and be sent out into the world, and really just have a very firsthand view of how the galaxy is changing. We're in this time of prosperity and it is a high moment in the Republic, but that also means that when things don't go well it's very striking and it's very sudden for them to realize their own vulnerability, their own place in the world. They have to actually take action to be a part of that, whether that means through investigation or just being friends to each other, or actually being in the middle of combat and war. All those different things are explored.

That's the larger piece, but then we have Lula, a young Padawan who is very invested in the Jedi Order and becoming the greatest Jedi that she can possibly be. We also have her really good friend Farzala, who's kind of mischievous. Then they make friends with other people along the way. It's a really exciting adventure story to write, and it's great to follow these characters and get to have an interaction with some old favorites and new friends along the way.

Charles, you're launching it all with *Light of the Jedi*. What's it like to be setting up this era?

Soule: Well, it's an honor and a privilege, as they say. It's also

incredibly terrifying and pressure-filled, but it's a job that I'm very excited to have. Obviously, the good thing about it is that all the ideas in *Light of the Jedi* come from all the discussions that we've been having over the last two years. It's great to have this team to draw on. Yes, I'm writing it, but we're all in it together. We all kick ideas around, and everybody's helping to make it as strong as it can be. I think that's true of all the projects, which has been really great.

As far as writing it, the job of this project, because it is the first one out of the gate, is to introduce this time period to the readers in a very specific way—to make it clear that this is different from *Star Wars* that we've seen before. At the same time, the book needs to deliver a very exciting action story, introduce a ton of Jedi like Avar Kriss, and a load of really cool people from the Republic like the chancellor I mentioned earlier, while at the same time introduce the Nihil—the villains of the piece who will be causing a lot of trouble. As I mentioned earlier, the High Republic is a very optimistic, idealistic society that believes the wind is at their back, and that they're going to be able to do great things in the galaxy. Not everybody agrees with that, and they have some huge things to overcome; that's the Nihil. It really goes to some cool places.

Finally, Cavan, you're writing the *Star Wars: The High Republic* series for Marvel Comics. What are the challenges that your characters will be facing?

Scott: Like Daniel, I'm excited because we're telling the story of a team of Jedi. You normally only see the Jedi going off in twos, but this is a proper group of Jedi who are working together, and it's all based around Keeve Trennis. She's a very capable Jedi. Unlike Reath, she really wants to get out there, so she's very excited when she's posted to Starlight. But she also doesn't feel worthy to be there.

Keeve finds herself surrounded by this group of Jedi who are all legendary figures. You've got Avar Kriss, who Charles introduces in his book first of all. Everyone thinks she's the best of the best, and Keeve is absolutely in awe of her. You've got a Trandoshan Jedi, Sskeer, who's been around seemingly forever and is really grumpy. You have Maru, who meditates through multitasking and is constantly surrounded by datapads lying around him. Then you have a pair of siblings, Terec and Ceret, that share one mind between them. Keeve has to keep up with all these people, and so she struggles completely through all of that. But again, it's all about how the characters work together and the lessons they can learn from each other, including how to be a Jedi in service in the best way.

04 Cover image for Justina Ireland's *A Test of Courage*

05

You have already mentioned the Nihil as a foe, but are they the only villains your various characters will face?

Scott: The Drengir are a species of sentient carnivorous plant creatures who spore over a certain section of the galaxy, near the frontier where our characters are. Throughout all of this, as we've been saying, the High Republic is our Camelot, and with that we mean both Arthurian Camelot and also 1960s Americana. But obviously, just like in both those eras, they hit problems early on. It's about how these Jedi and the Republic members cope with them.

On one side you've got the Nihil, who are these pirate raiders, and on the other side you've got this creeping horror that no one really understands. Are they just beasts? We know they're vegetation, but they seem to be spreading throughout the population, through planets. They're popping up here, there and everywhere, and we don't know at first if they are sentient, whether they have a reason to be doing what they're doing. It's seeding, every pun intended, distrust and fear in that frontier at a time where everyone has been saying it's all going to be okay. It's exciting to be dealing with some of the threats that no one even expected.

Gray: One thing that seems great about this mysterious station is that it's so lush with plant life. It's almost like this oasis in the middle of the galaxy. But they don't quite realize that the Drengir are there. The reasons why they don't know that and how the Drengir wound up on that station are all in the final third of the book, so I'm really loath to talk too much about it.

Soule: Claudia, that space station sounds super cool. Has that popped up anywhere else?

Gray: It has shown up before, so comic readers have already seen it and they may recognize it.

In conclusion, which two words would you use to describe each of your stories?

Soule: Badass and grand.

Older: Dangerous shenanigans.

Ireland: Space hijinks.

Gray: Surprising spacestation.

Scott: Epic and personal.

05 The authors with the Lucasfilm Story Group and Publishing teams at Skywalker Ranch.